Famous Fables for Little Troupers

Retold by
Greta Barclay Lipson, Ed. D.
The University of Michigan – Dearborn

Illustrated by Susan Kropa

Cover by Susan Kropa

Copyright © Good Apple, Inc., 1984

ISBN No. 0-86653-202-1

Printing No. 98765432

GOOD APPLE, INC.
BOX 299
CARTHAGE, IL 62321-0299

DEDICATION

For my dearest father, Joe Barclay, who built that big old house on a country road called Lake Promenade in Long Branch overlooking Lake Ontario. It was in that house, upstairs in the unoccupied rooms, that I found a memorable stage for the creative drama of my childhood. With my cousin Edna, I became a make-believe sophisticated French woman, elegantly dressed and in command of fluent, rapid-fire French which was the savored language of our fantasy. We were, Edna and I, two actors—finely attuned to one another like musicians in duet—resonating to each improvisational twist, with only ourselves for an audience.

* * * * * * * * * * * * * * * * * *

With appreciation to little sister Geraldine, who has helped with this book in incalculable ways. She has read and corrected and argued with an ardent and deep sense of the task, while respecting the defects of the writer. For her knowledge of the craft, her spirited intellect and her feisty humor, I thank her.

FAMOUS FABLES FOR LITTLE TROUPERS

TABLE OF CONTENTS | PAGE

PROVERB

WHAT IS A FABLE?

"The fable in those early times was not a child's plaything. It was a nation's primer."[1]

By definition a fable is a short, compact story, the essence of which is a moral, a point or a truism. There is, in these stories, a charming forthright and colorful representation of the foibles of human behavior that is simple to understand. The message is effective in its brevity. It is especially entertaining whether expressed by foolish people or animals as they go about their daily lives at work, at play, or at some nefarious business.

I have chosen the fables for many reasons. After 2500 years they have clearly withstood the test of time. Like the proverbial "sour grapes"--Aesop's maxims have flavored our colloquial language with little awareness on our part of our debt to him.

These pithy stories were created by learned people in ancient times and were the popular currency of the day. Yet the homespun wisdom and sharp edge of the stories appealed to the common folk as well. Always embraced warmly by children, these tales continue to speak to all of us today. Fables are old friends. Their messages are timeless, and the strengths and weaknesses they portray are recognizable as they remind us pungently of what it means to be human.

---

[1] AESOP'S FABLES, Illustrated Junior Library, Drawings by Fritz Kredel, Grosset & Dunlap, Inc., c 1947, p. xiv.

CREATIVE DRAMA: A DEFINITION

"The 4 basic requirements for the art of creative dramatics include a group of children, a qualified leader or teacher, a space large enough for children to move about freely and an idea from which to create." [2]

Creative drama is not intended for an audience. It is intended as a valuable and immediate experience for the players. Its purpose is to enrich, entertain, and refine cognitively and aesthetically. There are no lines to be memorized, there are no arduous rehearsals, there are no elaborate settings. If they choose, the children may use props that are simple and fun. The play is improvisational and intimate--performed for the benefit of the young players and their classmates. And best of all, everyone may participate since the purpose is not to showcase talent for the few, but to enjoy the pleasure of group participation with open casting. Anyone--boy or girl--can take any part. The story is different with each playing. A fool may later be a wise person, a king's part may become a queen's part, a beggar may later be a person of power and wisdom and a hero in one interpretation may turn out to be a villain in the next. Creative drama, at its best, is a flexible, ongoing social experience. When children express themselves in creative drama, they are making personal statements from their own perceptions about life, people and events.

---

[2] Geraldine Brain Siks, CREATIVE DRAMATICS: An Art for Children, Harper & Row, Inc., 1958, p. 21.

GUIDELINES FOR PLAYACTING

The starting point or beginning idea for these plays comes from Aesop's Fables. In these simple stories the conventional storytelling narrative with dialogue has been favored over the script form with specific parts. This allows for more creative drama. Many more interpretations and nuances are possible within the comfort of a familiar story. If a narrator is desired, permit the child to move in and out of the action as both narrator and character. He or she can be both inside and outside the play. The narrator offers background information or describes the setting, or reveals innermost thoughts. Then, the child, in the role of the actor, slips into the dialogue. With this approach to playacting the narrator is a pivotal person who gives life and flesh to a story, helps look inside the characters, and also assumes a role.

The teacher, as the leader, should feel comfortable about taking a role in the play to illustrate new directions or to model a part. Such participation in the drama with young children and older children is wonderfully effective.

Steps in the plan for creative drama with the class would be to:

1. Set the mood and read the story for pleasure.

2. Discuss the story thoroughly and reread it.

3. Examine the characters and action.

4. Discuss the point of the story.

5. Plan the dramatization with the class. Don't rush.

6. Ask for volunteers and cast the story.

7. Brainstorm for prop ideas if students want them.

8. Play just a favorite scene or the entire story.

9. Show appreciation with positive remarks.

10. Evaluate the experience.

11. Discuss--then change, add, or delete characters or events.

12. Rerun the story, replay it with other actors--today, tomorrow, or in the future.

Allow for a request time through the weeks, since nothing is quite so sweet as a familiar tale retold.

STORY DRAMATIZATION

Creative drama is central to story dramatization. This form of playacting has the same spontaneous and extemporaneous qualities as creative drama, but reaches beyond into a higher level of expression. In story dramatization there are present the "structure" of the story or the guidelines of the original story as the children have heard it read. Though they may choose to change the events of a story, or introduce new characters, or modify the ending--there still remains the security of a beginning, a middle and an end, to which all the children were initially introduced by the storyteller. Stories that are short, familiar, and full action are ideal. Those stories that lend themselves to additional characters and do not feature one person are best for fuller participation.

ABOUT AESOP

Who was the legendary person called Aesop, whose greatness we acknowledge twenty-five centuries after his death? Whether he was real or mythical, the life and background of this man are represented by many different accounts. However, there are some general points of agreement by scholars. He was born in 620 B.C. in Phrygia and was later taken to the Greek Island of Samos. It is said that he died violently at about the age of 56 in 564 B.C. He was a Greek slave who was distinguished by his exceptional intelligence and wit. Aesop was memorable both physically and intellectually. He suffered the unsightly impairment of a deformed back and was exceedingly unattractive--with his flat nose, misshapen head and strange facial features.

This unusual man was owned by several different masters in Samos. The last of these was Iadmon, who is said to have given Aesop his freedom out of admiration for his brilliance. As a free man Aesop travelled widely and became known for his skill as a storyteller and a social critic. Aesop had great wisdom, but these were not times of free speech. It would have been perilous to express one's opinion openly. Like the teachers, philosophers, scientists and politicians of his day, Aesop used the popular beast tales to make social statements. His audiences were kings and queens and ordinary people, all of whom listened and laughed as they recognized themselves and others.

Aesop was not the originator of the fables; indeed, these stories derived from ancient India and many Eastern nations. But as news of Aesop's incisive wit spread, the most memorable of the tales were attributed to him, for he was the master of the form. He was known to use the stories to illustrate a point persuasively or to win an argu-

ABOUT AESOP

ment. There are even accounts of where he told particular stories and for what purposes. It is believed that Aesop recited "The Frogs Asking for a King" to warn the citizens of Athens that a known tyrant (like Pisistratus, whom they feared) was better than an unknown ruler. It is seen in such examples that the fables were more than entertainment. They were used popularly as a forceful technique to persuade and influence public opinion.

There are at least two versions of how Aesop died: In his travels, he was accepted into the court of King Croesus of Lydia, where his status as philosopher and instructor became renowned. The King appointed Aesop as Ambassador of the Court, and it was in this capacity that he was sent to the city of Delphi. Aesop arrived with a large sum of money which was payment due to the citizens. Aesop, however, believed that the people were not worthy of this money and steadfastly refused to carry out this mission. The citizens were incensed with his imperious behavior and in their outrage set upon him. They took him forcibly to a place outside the city and threw him off the edge of a high cliff to his death below.

In another version, Aesop was falsely accused of the theft of a golden cup from the Delphian's Temple of Apollo. The religious article was found in his personal belongings, where it had been placed by the real culprit. Aesop tried valiantly to vindicate himself and even told the people the story of "The Eagle and the Beetle" as a plea to their hospitality. Sadly, he failed and was sentenced by the guardians of the temple to his fateful end.

ABOUT AESOP

Like so many great teachers and thinkers, Aesop suffered an ignominious end, but his wisdom endured. Following his death, the Delphians, overcome with bad times, regretted their heinous act against the old sage and offered reparation for his death. They gave the money for "Aesop's blood" to the grandson of Iadmon, the master who had freed the great slave.

Interestingly, Aesop himself never wrote down the tales he told, but three centuries following his death, the founder of the Alexandria Library gathered and wrote down 200 fables under the title ASSEMBLIES OF AESOPIC TALES. This collection was lost but served as the basis for another famous collection by Phaedrus who, during the time of Augustus Caesar in the early Christian era, turned the fables into Latin verses. Six hundred years after Aesop's death, Valerius Babrius combined Aesop's fables with a collection of ancient Indian beast tales. This was followed by the most definitive book of fables. It emerged in the year 1300, was written in Latin, and compiled by Maximus Planudes, a monk in Constantinople. These charming tales then circulated throughout Europe in every language on the continent.

Finally, as if by magic, the fables spread to people throughout the entire world. The tales bear the imprimatur of many collectors and translators of all religions and cultures. From Aristophenes and Socrates to Mark Twain,[3] the stories have been used as the basis for literature. They are at once important as literature, as art, and as social commentary, but most of all as pure delightful entertainment.

---

[3] Mark Twain credits "The Celebrated Jumping Frog of Calaveras County" to Aesop's tale of "The Athenian and the Frog." From: HOW TO TELL A STORY AND OTHER ESSAYS, WORKS, LITERARY ESSAYS, Author's National Edition, by Mark Twain (Samuel L. Clemens), New York: Harper & Brothers, c 1897.

THE BELLY AND THE OTHER MEMBERS
Cooperation Is Important

THE BELLY AND THE OTHER MEMBERS

CAST OF CHARACTERS:

Hand and Arms
Legs
Eyes
Mouth
Belly

A long time ago, before any of us can remember, the body parts did not work very well together. They grumbled and complained a great deal. They all had separate jobs to do and felt put upon because they were all obliged to feed the belly.

"How unfair!" they all thought.

"We spend so much of our precious day gathering goodies and all kinds of tasty foods for the belly that we barely have enough time for ourselves," lamented the hands and arms.

"You are not the only ones, you know," protested the legs. "If it were not for me walking around and about all over the land, you would have nothing to gather to feed that lazy belly!"

THE BELLY AND THE OTHER MEMBERS

"And do none of you consider that it is I--this pair of eyes--that shows you the way to all the places you walk to and all that food you gather for the nourishment of the belly?"

"Well!" said the mouth loudly, announcing his importance, "Where would the lot of you be without me to bite the food with my teeth and work it around with my tongue and send it on to its proper way to the belly?"

But, alas, no one answered anyone. They were all wrangling and quite angry with these services which they performed for the belly.

"As far as I can see, the belly is a no-account, lazy do-nothing organ," said the eyes, joined by the others.

"Let him just hang in there."

"Nobody has ever thanked me for all the hard work I've done."

"He can't even say a word without me," said the mouth.

And so they talked things over rather heatedly among themselves and came to a firm decision. No longer would they be fools and contribute to this lazy belly. He did nothing in return, and they were annoyed beyond endurance.

THE BELLY AND THE OTHER MEMBERS

"You can depend upon me. No more seeking out food by looking this way and that," said the eyes.

"I'm through walking over hill and dale to do this thankless job," said the legs.

"And you won't catch me gathering," said the arms.

"Nor pushing food in," said the hands, with digust.

"If ever I take another morsel in," said the mouth, "I hope all my teeth rot and fall from my head."

And so these body parts, foolishly thinking themselves all to be independent, held firm to their promises and none of them--not one--fed the belly. It is easy to imagine what happened. The lack of food in the belly made the legs grow thin and spindly. They could barely hold the weight of the body. The arms and hands, too, were near to the bone, and the muscles withered and could not work. The eyes were cloudy with fever and weakness and could not view the world with any clearness of sight. Even the mouth, now sunken and silent, could hardly move when it was time to discuss this desperate plight.

THE BELLY AND THE OTHER MEMBERS

The poor weakened members assembled in a circle for a meeting. Oh, but they looked to be a most pathetic lot! Their voices were barely audible.

"It is good that you are all here dear friends," whispered the mouth, opening the meeting.

"I fear we have been sorely mistaken," said another.

"We have judged our situation wrongly."

"Surely this proves that we cannot all go our separate ways."

"All of us must help one another for the good of our membership."

"Clearly, we depend upon one another for our very existence."

"The belly is slow and quiet, except when it gurgles, but still it does an important job to help keep us alive."

"This proves that each of us needs the others, and we must all work together."

And they did--as they all joined in a body for the common good.

The Point of the Story: Cooperation is important.

Ideas to Dramatize or Discuss

1. If you could add to, or change a part of the body, what would it be? Consider an offensive spray, like a skunk uses to discourage enemies, or a third eye in the back of your head. Can you demonstrate how a new body part would work?
2. Have the belly, who is silent in this version, make an appeal to the other members as it begins to feel the pain of hunger.
3. Allow the members to act out and express their physical changes as they grow weaker.
4. Report the incident of this conflict on the evening news. How would the commentary sound?
5. Assign a role to the brain in the play. What would its personality be and what would its attitude be toward the others?
6. At the conclusion of the play, have the stomach and the other members assemble together on chairs, stools or tables in positions which illustrate their places in the body.
7. What can you remember about a time at home or school when cooperation was very important and helped get a job done?

Props to Use

Have actors wear signs identifying their characters. Post signs for any other information when needed to help the play.

= A nylon stocking mask for the **stomach**
= A cardboard box to isolate the **stomach**, as it sits alone
= Big sunglasses for the **eyes**
= Lipstick for the **mouth**
= Big gloves for the **hands and arms**
= Heavy socks or leg warmers for the **legs**

My Name _____

SHOWTIME SKILLS

THE NAME OF THE PLAY WAS _____
_____

CHARACTERS IN THE PLAY: ACTED BY:

_____   _____
_____   _____
_____   _____
_____   _____
_____   _____

• •

THE PLAY MADE ME FEEL _____
_____
_____

I LIKED IT BEST WHEN _____
_____
_____

MY FAVORITE CHARACTER WAS _____
_____

I LIKED THIS CHARACTER BECAUSE _____
_____

A DIFFERENT TITLE COULD BE _____
_____

IF I COULD CHANGE THE ENDING, I WOULD _____
_____

VENUS AND THE CAT
Don't Try to Be Something You Are Not

VENUS AND THE CAT

CAST OF CHARACTERS:

Felinea - the cat
Tillie - her friend
Venus - Goddess of Love
Selwyn Kipper - the Groom
Minister
Friends

It is a known fact that once there was a very homely stray cat who lived among the poorer houses in the back streets of a town. She owned nothing and wanted nothing, for she lived near a fish market and found all the nourishment she needed to keep body and soul together. The only thing that she could truly call her own was her name. She could not remember who had named her but she was proud of her name, for it had the sound of one who enjoyed a much higher station in life than she. Her name was Felinea.

VENUS AND THE CAT

One day, perched on her favorite fence in the entire neighborhood, she confided to her orange-headed cat friend, Tillie, "I have seen other cats who are pampered and groomed. They wear ribbons and bells and fancy collars. They live in fine houses and sit in the laps of privileged ladies and gentlemen, who stroke them with fingers heavy with jeweled rings, but..." The sentence trailed into space as Felinea's eyes misted over.

"But what?" demanded Tillie irritably. "Are you going to tell me you wouldn't care to live like that?" Tillie was always sarcastic and nasty.

"Yes," said Felinea, "in a word that is what I am telling you. I want my independence. I don't want anyone to own me. My freedom means too much to me."

"Then what are you complaining about?" Tillie posed the question as she jumped down to forage through the refuse freshly dumped by the neighbors.

11

VENUS AND THE CAT

"I am not complaining, but I must confess to you that I long to be loved. I want to love someone who will love me back," Felinea sighed.

"Well, you can't have everything," Tillie reminded her. "We have the best fish market in these parts, and for us it is open all night. It is just a stone's throw from any part of town. I know cats who would forfeit eight of their nine lives for such luxury!"

"It's not that I'm ungrateful," Felinea apologized. "I just think there may be more to life."

Tillie was exhausting her patience. "Who do you think you are anyway--a royal princess? You had better straighten out, Ms. Cat." Since there was no answer from Felinea, the orange-haired cat persisted, "What do you say we take a trip to the fish market? My stomach tells me we are approaching the supper hour." And so the two cats bestirred themselves, jumped from their perch on the fence, and moved gracefully in the direction of their favorite dining place.

VENUS AND THE CAT

"What is your pleasure, Madam?" Tillie asked in her attempt to humor her friend. "Would you have the head of a herring, the belly of a carp, or a delicate catfish?"

There was no response. Tillie looked mischievously in the direction of her friend. Felinea seemed in a trance. "Pray tell, what is your problem? You seem so still and dazed."

Felinea's whiskers twitched. "I have found my one to love," she sighed.

"Who might that be? I see no other cat around."

"Oh no, dear Tillie. It is not a cat I love. It is a fishmonger who stands at that stall filling his pushcart with fish."

"What madness is that?" asked Tillie, disbelieving.

"Can't you see?" said Felinea. "He has hair like golden flax with ringlets falling on his brow. His eyes are azure blue like our most aristocratic Siamese. His lips are of pale pink and his teeth white enough to match the very best of ours." She paused from her long litany. "I believe I have truly found my beloved."

VENUS AND THE CAT

What followed through the days ahead were torturous for pathetic Felinea. She tailed the handsome lad wherever he took his wares. But never, ever was he seen to give a glance in her direction. Of course, one could expect no more. She, however, loved him madly. So zealously did she pine and long for him that one strange and memorable day Venus, the goddes of love, came to her!

"You have yearned so deeply and sincerely for the love of this young lad that I have come to answer your fervent prayers. It is against my better judgment, but I am prepared to turn you into a fair maiden so that you can win his love. But I must warn you to be careful of your deportment. You will be watched day and night for any embarrassing transgressions. If you do not change your ways as a cat--you will be punished."

And so it happened that Felinea (who by the way retained her name) was transformed into a young woman and promptly introduced herself to the comely fishmonger.

VENUS AND THE CAT

"Hello. My name is Felinea."

"Good morning. My name is Selwyn Kipper. Do you like fish?"

"I love fish," the charming girl answered sincerely. It seemed their conversation would never cease since they shared so many common interests.

"I love you," the young Kipper said.

"I love you and have always loved you from afar," Felinea blushed as she revealed her heart.

"Marry me," said Selwyn Kipper.

"With pride, I do accept," she gratefully consented.

A minister was called and married the happy twosome in a simple but solemn ceremony. The maiden wore a bridal veil of delicate ivory. Her gown was modest but in the fashion of the day. Her bouquet was a fragile cluster of spring flowers with upturned faces.

VENUS AND THE CAT

The young Mr. Kipper's friends were present at the ceremony. They complimented the bride and shook the hand of the groom. They threw rice and hailed the new marriage. But best of all these caring friends decorated the wagon to be used by the newlyweds in their departure. It was replete with flowers. It had a sign for all the townspeople to see which read in bold script **JUST MARRIED!** Oh, this was indeed a

a happy time, and heaven smiled on Felinea and Selwyn. The wagon departed, trundling through town. The bride's veil billowed with the wind, as they embarked toward their destination--when--all at once a tragedy occurred.

With her excellent eyes, Felinea saw a mouse. He was only a small inconsequential little fellow to be sure. But nonetheless, in the heart of a cat it was worth a chase. Felinea's juices flowed as all her energy was riveted upon the mouse. Forgetting all that she had gone through to win her love--Felinea jumped off the wagon while it was still in motion, chased after that mouse and gave him a good trouncing.

That is sadly the conclusion of the story. Venus, the goddess of love, made her justice swift and sure. "Since you cannot help acting like a cat--then you shall be a cat once again."

Alas, this is the way the marriage of Felinea and Selwyn Kipper came to an end.

VENUS AND THE CAT

Everyone wondered who she was--this very homely stray cat--who wore a bridal veil of delicate ivory and sat upon the favored fence of all the cats in town.

The Point of the Story: Don't try to be something you are not.

Ideas to Dramatize or Discuss

1. Occasionally Felinea starts to "meow" when she is having a conversation with people. How does it sound and how do people react?
2. Tillie, the orange-haired cat, interrupts the wedding ceremony and tries to tell the truth about the new bride.
3. While the groom and the wedding guests are eating wedding cake after the ceremony, Felinea starts to eat raw fish to everyone's amazement.
4. The groom, Selwyn Kipper, surprises Felinea with a present. He brings home a very big dog who thinks he recognizes Felinea but isn't sure. Act out this frightening scene.
5. Selwyn's mother, Mrs. Kipper, Senior, is knitting from a large ball of colorful wool as she and Felinea talk together in the parlor. The former cat cannot keep her eyes off the wool. What happens?
6. Cat friends of Felinea sit on the fence outside the window and sing a chorus of songs, begging her to come out and play. What does she do? How does she explain this attention to Selwyn?
7. The new mayor wants to get rid of all the stray cats in town. Felinea goes to the meeting at the city hall, as a girl, to object to this cleanup. What does she say and how is it received?
8. Did you ever wish you were someone else? Whom would you want to be and why?

Props to Use

Have actors wear signs identifying their characters. Post signs for any other information when needed to help the play.

= Wigs, or saucy women's hats, for Felinea and Tillie
= Eyebrow pencil whiskers and eye makeup for the cats
= Work shirt, cap, kerchief, boots for Selwyn Kipper
= Curtain bridal gown and veil for Felinea
= Cardboard box wagon or wagon made of assembled chairs
= "Just Married!" sign to tie onto the wagon
= Newspapers for wrapping fish
= Painted backdrop of a marketplace with stalls for vendors
= Reversed collar for the minister

My Name _____

SHOWTIME SKILLS

THE NAME OF THE PLAY WAS _____
_____

CHARACTERS IN THE PLAY: ACTED BY:

_____   _____
_____   _____
_____   _____
_____   _____
_____   _____

* *

THE PLAY MADE ME FEEL _____
_____
_____

I LIKED IT BEST WHEN _____
_____
_____

MY FAVORITE CHARACTER WAS _____
_____
_____

I LIKED THIS CHARACTER BECAUSE _____
_____
_____

A DIFFERENT TITLE COULD BE _____
_____
_____

IF I COULD CHANGE THE ENDING, I WOULD _____
_____
_____

THE LION AND HIS THREE WISE ADVISORS
A Wise Person Knows When to Say Nothing

THE LION AND HIS THREE WISE ADVISORS

CAST OF CHARACTERS:

Lion
Lion's wife
Sheep ⎫
Donkey ⎬   Advisors
Fox ⎭

The lion, as we all know, is the King of the Beasts. Like all kings he gave a lot of speeches and roared a great deal. On many of these occasions his wife began to notice something that no one else would tell him.

"Your breath," she said, "is simply awful. How can you expect to do all that roaring in public with such a foul breath?"

The lion, who was not accustomed to being told the truth, was really very angry with the frankness of his bold queen. "It is very strange," he growled, "that no one else has ever complained of such a thing."

THE LION AND HIS THREE WISE ADVISORS

"Now really, your majesty," she said with impatience, "do you believe that just any of the subjects living in your kingdom could possibly think it would be safe to tell you such an unpleasant fact about yourself?"

By this time the king was roaring mad. "I know what I will do to prove you wrong," said he to his mate. "I will call my three wise advisors here and ask for their honest opinion. I have always been able to depend upon them in good times and bad." No sooner did the idea pass his lips than his three wise advisors were standing in his presence, with their brows furrowed, waiting to hear what important matters of state he had to discuss with them.

"Now then, dear madam," he said to the sheep. "Would you step forward and give me your ear since I have a matter of great importance to impart to you?" The sheep, as the king's woolly advisor, did as she was bidden. She approached seriously.

The king started talking more closely to the poor sheep's nose than to her ear as he shared this matter of deep interest. "Would you say that my breath is bad?" he asked.

THE LION AND HIS THREE WISE ADVISORS

The sheep staggered backward, almost in a swoon from the experience of being so close to the lion's mouth. She tried desperately to regain her control as she assured her leader, "Why no, your majesty. There is no way in the world that I would say that your breath is bad!"

But everyone could see that the lion was displeased with this judgment. "Then why do you fall back as if in a faint when I speak so closely to you? For whatever the reason may be," he said threateningly, "you must be lying." Without any official warning, the great lion leaped upon the creature, and in a flash he bit off the head of his first hapless advisor.

"And now," he said, turning to his second advisor, the donkey, "I need your sincere and thoughtful opinion on a matter of great importance." The donkey approached his monarch haltingly, but all the while his eyes had taken in the scene. He saw the dead sheep carcass and knew from all signs that whatever passed between himself and the lion would require more wisdom than he had ever before mustered.

THE LION AND HIS THREE WISE ADVISORS

"Do you believe," bellowed the agitated lion, "that I have foul-smelling breath?" His words were carried on the air, directly into the face of the donkey who was altogether unprepared for this event.

The donkey's eyes watered and clouded his vision as the monarch's breath sent its message to his tender and very sensitive nose. Now indeed he knew what happened to the dead sheep and would at all costs avoid a similar fate for himself. "Let me assure you, my majesty," he answered quickly, trying valiantly to recover himself, "your breath is as sweet as the lilacs in springtime." He smiled a cheap and lying smile as he shook his head to deny the suggestion that his monarch's breath was bad.

"Then why," raged the lion, "do your eyes water so heavily? You could barely see what you were about or which way to turn away from my royal presence."

Nothing the donkey could say would save him from his destiny. And as before, the lion fell upon the confused donkey accusing him of being a flatterer. Demanding that he pay the penalty for his dishonesty, the lion tore the donkey limb from limb.

THE LION AND HIS THREE WISE ADVISORS

Once again the lion made his opening statement--this time to the fox who was his last remaining advisor. He betrayed no anger and was cool and composed. He did not want to alarm the fox who was, by this time, unsettled by his royal anger. "I have some earnest concerns to discuss with you, wise fox. Join me more closely so that you may hear what these may be."

The fox was cautious and came as close as she dared. The lion exhaled deeply before proceeding and then asked loudly, "Would you say, in your esteemed judgment, that my breath is foul?" He blew his vapors throughout the room.

THE LION AND HIS THREE WISE ADVISORS

Deftly, with the hand of a magician, the fox pulled forth a large white handkerchief. From where it came so suddenly no one could tell. She flourished it with a grand eloquence, and as she coughed and sneezed and sniffled noisily, she covered her mouth and nose with mannerly care. "I regret most profoundly," she said sincerely, "that my cold is so miserable that I can in no way smell the difference between a flower and a skunk. Do forgive me your majesty."

The Point of the Story: A wise person knows when to say nothing.

THE LION AND HIS THREE WISE ADVISORS

Ideas to Dramatize or Discuss

1. The fox decides that the cook is causing the lion's bad breath by adding too much garlic to the lion's food. Call the cook in to explain.
2. The royal dentist is called in to examine the lion's mouth. She comes in with frightening tools.
3. The king hears a singing commercial for mouthwash. Write a commercial for a group and have them sing it.
4. A child, who always tells the truth, is called into the lion's court. What will the child say? How will the lion respond?
5. An inventor brings in her electronic deflector which bounces the lion's bad breath back to him.
6. The lion is angry with graffiti on a wall which he passes on a trip to town. The inscriptions say uncomplimentary things about his bad behavior with his advisors and the evils of power.
7. Have the king or queen interview new candidates for the jobs left open by the donkey and the sheep. Who would want such a job anyway?
8. Can you remember a time when you wished that you had kept your mouth shut? Tell about the incident.

Props to Use

Have actors wear signs identifying their characters. Post signs for any other information when needed to help the play.

= Eyebrow pencil for the lion's whiskers on the King and Queen
= A long white woolly sweater for the sheep
= A homemade tail for the donkey
= An old felt or straw hat with holes cut out for donkey ears
= A big hanky or kerchief for the fox's nose
= Aluminum foil crowns
= A bottle of mouthwash from the Queen

My Name _____

SHOWTIME SKILLS

THE NAME OF THE PLAY WAS _____
_____

CHARACTERS IN THE PLAY: ACTED BY:

_____   _____

_____   _____

_____   _____

_____   _____

_____   _____

• •

THE PLAY MADE ME FEEL _____
_____
_____

I LIKED IT BEST WHEN _____
_____
_____

MY FAVORITE CHARACTER WAS _____
_____
_____

I LIKED THIS CHARACTER BECAUSE _____
_____
_____

A DIFFERENT TITLE COULD BE _____
_____
_____

IF I COULD CHANGE THE ENDING, I WOULD _____
_____
_____

JUPITER, NEPTUNE, MINERVA AND MOMUS
It Is Easy to Criticize

JUPITER, NEPTUNE, MINERVA AND MOMUS

CAST OF CHARACTERS:

Jupiter - a god
Neptune - a god
Minerva - a goddess
Momus - a god
Bull
Person

In ancient times the gods lived among the heavenly clouds and luminous stars on a beautiful mountain high above the earth. They drank fragrant wine and ate delicious ambrosia, but they were bored with their privileged existence and were often in search of pleasant diversions and mischief to occupy themselves. On one such day, Neptune, the god of the sea, and Minerva, the goddess of wisdom, fell to arguing about who could create the most perfect thing in existence. The gods were all very vain and forever determined to prove their superiority.

JUPITER, NEPTUNE, MINERVA AND MOMUS

"I do not know at this moment what it is that I would create," Neptune said. "But I do know beyond a doubt that anything I put my hand to will be an awesome object for all to cherish and admire." He turned his back haughtily away from Minerva and folded his arms as if to bring the conversation to a close.

JUPITER, NEPTUNE, MINERVA AND MOMUS

"One moment there!" Minerva shouted in return. "Does your arrogance know no limits? You do not know what your precious object will be and already you act as if you are the winner! I am a rare and gifted goddess whose skills cannot be matched. I would most likely reduce you to shame with the grandeur of my invention."

"And what of me?" boomed Jupiter, jumping into the fray. "It is I who have the greatest power of all in the universe. It is I who send my thunderbolts to earth and rend the atmosphere with the fury of my strength! There can be no doubt that it is I, the all powerful one, who can produce the most perfect object to behold." He threw a thunderbolt to earth to emphasize the truth of his statement.

But Minerva and Neptune ignored him, for they had seen his act before and were not inclined to accept such authority. Nothing, it seemed, was settled--for each of them shouted louder than the other, and the heat of their dissension lit up the sky.

JUPITER, NEPTUNE, MINERVA AND MOMUS

"Come now," said Jupiter, who was the oldest and considered himself the wisest. "There is only one way that we can conclude this endless dispute." Minerva and Neptune paused to take a breath and were curious about this promised solution. "Let each of us create something new which has never, ever been seen before. Then we will show our work to someone who will judge our efforts."

"Yes, yes, I do like that," Minerva agreed quickly with uncommon sweet temper.

"Ah, yes," said Neptune with unusual good humor. "But who will be this judge of whom you speak? Who would dare to judge this contest?" For Neptune knew as well as the others that the power of each of them was fearsome to deal with when they were angered.

Jupiter responded, "There is such a one, by the name of Momus, who is himself a god. I believe and I hope he will be sensible and fair. He will act as our judge." Jupiter's decision was final. Each of the three turned around and set about making their own special projects in great secrecy.

The day came for judging. It was attended by great ceremony and curiosity.

JUPITER, NEPTUNE, MINERVA AND MOMUS

"Behold," Neptune announced with a sweep of his arm, as he entered. "I bring you an animal which I will call a bull. He is fashioned from my very own plan." It was indeed a surprise since no one had ever seen a bull before. It was an adult bovine animal which weighed 1500 pounds. "See this dazzling white bull with huge muscles that ripple beneath his rich coat."

The bull's voice boomed out of his chest in great rolls of sound as he bellowed deeply.

"Moo, moo, moo." He pawed the earth with restless hooves.

"Is he not a powerful and perfect creation?" asked Neptune.

"Oh no, oh no," said Momus shaking his head. "This is not perfection!"

"What could possibly be wrong with this extraordinary beast?" asked Neptune.

"It is his horns, of course," Momus pointed to the bull's head. "His horns are in the wrong place. They don't belong at the top of his head. They belong below his eyes so that when he attacks he can see what he is doing and appraise his nasty work."

JUPITER, NEPTUNE, MINERVA AND MOMUS

This left Neptune angrier than the bull.

"It's my turn now," Minerva announced clearly, as she drew the gods aside to witness her creation.

"And what may this thing be?" they all asked in a single voice.

"Why, it is a house to live in," she explained. The sun glistened off the structure's crystalline smoothness. It was indeed a surprise because no one had ever seen a house before. She glided into the shadows of the graceful portico. She stood in the coolness of the welcoming entryway and waited for the god's admiration.

"Is this house not a divine and a perfect creation?"

"Oh no, oh no," said Momus shaking his head. "This is not perfection."

"What could possibly be wrong with this elegant house?" Minerva demanded.

"This house needs wheels."

"Wheels!" she screamed.

"Yes, wheels," Momus answered. "It must be moved away if one's neighbors are troublesome and quarrelsome. How else can bad neighbors be left behind?" Minerva was in a fury.

Jupiter had been waiting for his turn most impatiently. He stepped forward and with royal finality he declared, "I, and only I, have created a person. It is a person so wondrous that all must come to see and pay me honor." He stepped back with a gesture of profound pride and awaited the sounds of praise for this marvel of invention. "It is straight, it is strong, it is intelligent. I myself assembled it in the image of the gods. Is this person not remarkable and a perfect creation?"

"Oh no, oh no," said Momus shaking his head. "This is not perfection."

"What could possibly be wrong with this creature of excellence?" Jupiter bellowed. "Never before in the knowledge of created things has such a one been made."

Momus chuckled and with a sneer he said, "This person needs a window in its chest! How else can we know its innermost feelings and thoughts without a glass for us to look through?"

JUPITER, NEPTUNE, MINERVA AND MOMUS

Jupiter was outraged and could no longer endure the criticism of this foolish Momus. He thought he would burst with anger.

"You cannot be pleased and are impossible to satisfy. This is bad! That is bad! Everything to you is bad! Tell us, if you will, what have you ever done that has been worthy of praise? You have done nothing, but still you find fault with others." With that outburst, Jupiter pointed his finger toward the door and his message was clear. He banished Momus from the home of the gods.

"Leave us forever and never return," commanded Jupiter.

As the mocking Momus left, he looked back and called to Minerva, "By the way, Minerva, I forgot to tell you that your sandals, which you deem so beautiful, make a comical squeak when you walk."

This last remark was to be expected, for Momus was the god of ridicule and censure. Like Momus, there are those who have never done anything important themselves but find it easy to criticize others. Some people never have a good word to say and can never be pleased.

The Point of the Story: It is easy to criticize.

Ideas to Dramatize or Discuss

1. Have Jupiter create a person in full view of the class, as he pretends to assemble a classmate. All the body parts should be fitted together and all the features painted and put into place on the face. The assembler should explain orally what is being done as the work takes place.

2. Act upon Momus's suggestion of putting a window in the chest of a person to see what the person is feeling. Tell us what someone who looked inside the creature might say.

3. At the right time in the drama have the whole class as a chorus say Momus's line, "Oh no, oh no, this is not perfection!"

4. Where might Minerva put a house with wheels if she followed the suggestion of Momus? Act out her decision. What will happen? Will she call a mobile home park?

5. At appropriate times have students make sound effects for thunderbolts, the sound of mooing for the bull, and the ringing of the doorbell on Minerva's house.

6. Astonish Momus. Have a volunteer invent a people machine with moving parts and sounds. Use other class members as the machine parts. Give good directions for movements and sounds. Let others try the same invention.

7. Introduce a red cape that is inadvertently waved in front of the bull's eyes during the drama. Expect the unexpected.

8. Has there been a time when you tried and tried to please someone but couldn't? Was this person a friend or someone in your family?

Props to Use

Have actors wear signs identifying their characters. Post signs for any other information when needed to help the play.

= A fool's paper hat for Momus
= Cotton beards for the gods and a long dress for Minerva
= Fancy towels or material on chairs for three thrones
= Boxes or cardboard for Minerva's house
= Crowns out of aluminum foil
= Cardboard thunderbolts to be thrown by Jupiter
= A brown stocking cap for the bull
= A hoop earring in the nose of the bull
= A full-length person traced and cut out of butcher paper or a stuffed dummy to represent Jupiter's person

SHOWTIME SKILLS

THE NAME OF THE PLAY WAS _____

_____

CHARACTERS IN THE PLAY: ACTED BY:

_____   _____

_____   _____

_____   _____

_____   _____

_____   _____

• •

THE PLAY MADE ME FEEL _____

_____

_____

I LIKED IT BEST WHEN _____

_____

_____

MY FAVORITE CHARACTER WAS _____

_____

_____

I LIKED THIS CHARACTER BECAUSE _____

_____

_____

A DIFFERENT TITLE COULD BE _____

_____

_____

IF I COULD CHANGE THE ENDING, I WOULD _____

_____

_____

THE CITY MOUSE AND THE COUNTRY MOUSE
It Is Better to Be Satisfied with Less and Live Happily

THE CITY MOUSE AND THE COUNTRY MOUSE

CAST OF CHARACTERS:

Tyrone - the city mouse
Elmer - the country mouse
House Dog
Family

It happened that two unlikely companions had made a plan to spend some time together. They were much different from each other because one was a country mouse, born and bred in the fields and in touch with nature, while the other was a town mouse raised up in the glitter and hubbub of the city.

Having consented to visit the country, the polished city mouse sat erect at the table of his poor cousin whose invitation he had accepted with hesitation. Dressed in the latest fashion, he tolerated the rough homespun napkin tucked into his ruffled shirt. He was never rude, for he genuinely cared about his poor relative always wishing him the very best.

THE CITY MOUSE AND THE COUNTRY MOUSE

"I do worry about you, Elmer--living in these crude and harsh surroundings."

"Please, Tyrone," said Elmer, the poor but gentle host. "Don't fret about me so. At this moment it is my wish to please you with the very best food I have to offer. It is so seldom that we have some time together."

As is the way of many who live poorly and are of modest means, Elmer set his table with all manner of wholesome country food in too great abundance. Feeling himself insecure and of low station, he rushed back and forth feverishly from pantry to table where his guest dined with such fine and gracious manners. "Do try the oats," Elmer entreated. "They have such a wholesome nutty flavor. Have some barley. The corn is especially golden and sweet this season. It comes right from the field to my table. And see the dewey green peas nuzzling in their pods just for your pleasure."

"Look here, dear fellow," said Tyrone, "It is not that I do not appreciate your hospitality. I really do. But you are living such a dull and miserable life out here in the backwoods. Won't you oblige me by coming to see the city just once? Come see where I live and let me introduce you to excitement, to luxury and to the ways of the world!"

Tyrone's blandishments were so sincere and persuasive that Elmer, the country mouse, said, "I am convinced by everything you have said. I am too good to live such a mean and meagre life." He packed his bag and they both set out for town.

THE CITY MOUSE AND THE COUNTRY MOUSE

What excitement there was to behold! "I don't believe what my eyes see," exclaimed Elmer. The lights were dazzling, the noise deafening, the horses and buggies were regal. With each new sight the country mouse stopped to look, to listen and to admire the people and the places.

"Come, come, my cousin. You are still only in the streets of the city. You have not even savored the luxury of my home," Tyrone admonished, dragging the innocent Elmer along by his paw. Soon they arrived at the home of the city mouse who pressed his humble companion to enter, "Please sit at a table which is unlike any you have ever seen."

"Everything you have told me is true," said little Elmer in admiration. "This velvet furniture, these polished hardwood floors, the lace curtains...I am overcome with the grandeur!"

"You must now sample from my menu." Tyrone proudly explained the source of every tasty morsel. "Here are parings from imported cheeses, scraps of roast beef and crumbs from freshly baked pastry. . . ."

THE CITY MOUSE AND THE COUNTRY MOUSE

Just then they were interrupted by noises from the family of the house. They were arriving late from the theatre. "What is that I hear?" gasped the country mouse.

"Hush--and they will soon leave for their upstairs rooms," reassured Tyrone. The mice dashed to a hiding place under the sink where they waited--their hearts beating fast with fear. The conversation of the humans was booming because they stood so close.

"Hello, what do we have here?"

"Do you think we have mice?"

"Yes, I do see signs of the little fellows."

"No matter, I'll attend to the traps tomorrow." Great footsteps came close, then moved away in giant shoes that could crush in a moment. Fading human voices were heard and then Tyrone spoke. "The coast is clear. It is their bedtime. There is no more cause for worry."

THE CITY MOUSE AND THE COUNTRY MOUSE

The two mice moved out hesitantly with a little less swagger. They talked softly, like civilized friends once again, and drank some tea when all at once, with no warning, a door swung open and a huge beast with a glistening collar came snarling toward them. The teeth of the brute flashed a warning, and the chase was on. This time they took refuge in a hole at the baseboard. But the dog's large moist nose poked and sniffed while they clutched one another and dared not breathe. The dog growled as her nails scratched at the molding as if to drag them out.

Mercifully the canine grew weary of the game and left. The mice listened to the tapping of her paws as she retreated and left them to peace and quiet.

Tyrone, accustomed to these life-threatening interruptions, was quickly restored to his former good humor. "Now, the very next thing I want to show you is...."

But Elmer would not let his host finish. "Enough, enough of this," the country mouse protested, as he leaned against the wall, his chest heaving with alarm from the dog's savage visit. "You may think I live like a rodent in a hole in my cottage, and perhaps I do. But you, dear sir, have far too much to fear. Horrible things await you around every corner. If this is the price you must pay for your life of luxury in the city, you are welcome to it. I am afraid I could not endure these conditions. I thank you for your good intentions, but I must bid you farewell and return to the quiet and security of my cottage in the fields."

The Point of the Story: It is better to be satisfied with less and live happily.

Ideas to Dramatize or Discuss

1. Reverse the situation in the story and have Tyrone, the city mouse, move into the quiet and safety of the country with Elmer. How would life be for both of them?
2. If Tyrone lived in a bakery shop instead of a grand house in town, how would that change the events in the story?
3. Where are some places that the two mice could run and hide other than under the sink or a hole in the baseboard? How could other places in the house lead them to further adventures?
4. Introduce into the story a strong and colorful circus mouse who does tricks for a living and travels from town to town. Which of the two--Elmer or Tyrone--would consider that a most appealing life?
5. What would happen to Elmer if he were separated from Tyrone on their arrival into the big and frightening city?
6. Have the mice follow some children on a path which leads them into a toy store. The mice have not seen mechanical toys before and they think they are real. What happens?
7. Did you ever wish you lived in someone else's house or in a different place? What was your choice and why?

THE CITY MOUSE AND THE COUNTRY MOUSE

Props to Use

Have actors wear signs identifying their characters. Post signs for any other information when needed to help the play.

= Bow ties, scarves and hats for the mice
= Duffle bags or knapsacks for both travellers
= Ruffled fancy collar for the well-dressed city mouse
= Napkins and cups on the table
= Assorted boxes and containers of food for the table
= Collar and leash for the dog
= Big shoes for the family members
= A table for the mice to hide under
= A backdrop of crowded stores on a city street

SHOWTIME SKILLS

THE NAME OF THE PLAY WAS _____
_____

CHARACTERS IN THE PLAY: ACTED BY:

_____   _____
_____   _____
_____   _____
_____   _____
_____   _____

* *

THE PLAY MADE ME FEEL _____
_____
_____

I LIKED IT BEST WHEN _____
_____
_____

MY FAVORITE CHARACTER WAS _____
_____
_____

I LIKED THIS CHARACTER BECAUSE _____
_____
_____

A DIFFERENT TITLE COULD BE _____
_____
_____

IF I COULD CHANGE THE ENDING, I WOULD _____
_____
_____

THE OLD WOMAN AND HER MAIDS
If You Are Too Smart, You May Outsmart Yourself

THE OLD WOMAN AND HER MAIDS

CAST OF CHARACTERS:

Old woman
Amy
Hattie ⎱ 3 maids
Mandy ⎰
Rooster

There was once an old woman who lived on a rich, working farm. One day she was heard to say to herself, "I really must have some help to work this farm. It would be good for me to travel to town and find some strong young women to board here and share the chores." No sooner did she hear herself make this pronouncement than she tied her bonnet on her white hair and walked slowly to town.

"Perhaps three young maidens will be just the right number. We can live together and work diligently in good humor, for there is nothing like hard work to keep one happy," she chuckled with conviction. Her opinion did not allow for people who did not share her attitude. She believed that hard work was the way to happiness. Her trip to town was a success, for she found the three maids of her choice quickly, since jobs were scarce in town.

THE OLD WOMAN AND HER MAIDS

As they all walked the dusty road back to the farm, the first girl, Amy, inquired, "What will my first job be, kind mistress? I have never worked on a farm before, but I am most willing!"

"Your job, dear Amy, will be to rise at 5:00 a.m., and milk the cow."

Amy groaned inwardly at the thought of awakening so early.

Hattie was the next to ask, "How will I help with the chores each day, my mistress? Farm work is new to me, but I am very anxious to learn."

"You will rise at 5:00 a.m., have a proper breakfast with your sisters, then hurry to the barnyard to feed the chickens and collect their eggs." Hattie attempted to conceal her dismay at the mention of that early hour.

Mandy, the last of the threesome, looked earnestly into the eyes of the old woman and posed the same question. "I know nothing of farms or farm creatures, but I am eager to learn. What will the first of my daily chores be?"

"Each day you will arise at 5:00 a.m. and eat breakfast. Your job will be to mix the leftover chicken feed with scraps from the table, stir it with milk from the cow, and then slop the pigs in the pen."

THE OLD WOMAN AND HER MAIDS

Mandy swallowed hard. She had never left her bed before the town clock struck nine, and to compound her misery hers sounded like the most unpleasant chore of all.

The walk took all of the them to the end of the road and the most cheery farm house that one could wish for. After a refreshing treat of hazelnut cookies and a pitcher of cool milk, the old lady showed them to their beds and bade them goodnight.

As they lay in the dark, they whispered through half the night and shared their disquiet and worries.

Amy was the first to express her concern. "Do you think that girls like us from the city will be successful on a farm?"

"I don't know but I hope the mistress will come to like us," was Hattie's concern.

"Will she be pleased with our work?" wondered Mandy.

"Can we really be happy here?"

"Though she explained our chores, will we know what we are doing?"

THE OLD WOMAN AND HER MAIDS

Daybreak found the young maids snuggled under their feather beds, deep in their sleep--dreaming the sweet dreams of youth, when all at once a deafening noise pierced the silence of the house. They sat bolt upright in bed, shocked and astonished.

"Cock-a-doodle-doo. There's no more sleep for you! Cock-a-doodle-doo."

"Up, up, up,--Amy, Hattie, Mandy," trilled the old lady as she rousted them out of bed to attend their morning chores.

"But it's so early," Hattie whined in disbelief, as the three of them rubbed their eyes and wandered drowsily on the cold wooden floor, bumping into each other trying to collect their wits.

"When my darling red rooster says 'arise' then we must all obey his command," the woman chuckled.

"Does she let the rooster run this household?" Mandy wailed, on her way to slop the pigs.

"How can we bear that raucous rooster?" Amy lamented, swinging her bucket on her way to milk the cow.

THE OLD WOMAN AND HER MAIDS

But endure it they did. Day after day after day they were torn from their rest, wee in the hours of the early morn, by the red feathered tyrant.

"Cock-a-doodle-doo. There's no more sleep for you!" He flapped his wings with power, for he knew he was cock of the walk. "No one sleeps, once I have risen."

After a time, a wicked plan began to hatch among the tired girls. They whispered together and the conspiracy was born.

"One of us must grab the rooster."

"We had better wait until he sleeps."

"I will gladly wring his neck and silence his clarion call, never to hear it again!"

And so they did. On one dark and moonless night they put him to rest forever. But the old lady missed her arrogant rooster with his morning call. So anxious was she to arise in time for chores that she woke the three girls earlier and earlier every day until they barely had any sleep at all. She was heard to walk the floor talking to herself.

THE OLD WOMAN AND HER MAIDS

"Is it time, I wonder, to awaken for the chores? Is it time to greet the new day?"

And so the girls were driven out of bed in the middle of each cold and shivery night. The pity was, you see, that the poor woman had no clock and without her adored rooster she really never knew when dawn broke. Oh, how desperately the maids regretted their deed, for they were much worse off now than they had ever been before.

"What have we done? What have we done?"

"How did we bring this misery upon ourselves?" they groaned as they staggered about and did the old lady's bidding in the middle of the night.

"There is no help for our weary bones."

For too late the maids now realized that their cunning had overreached itself. In truth, they had been so much better off when the fool rooster was alive to waken them with his "cock-a-doodle-doo."

The Point of the Story: If you are too smart, you may outsmart yourself.

Ideas to Dramatize or Discuss

1. A peddler comes by the farmhouse. He is selling a new-fangled item called an alarm clock. The woman and the girls have never seen such a thing. They listen to his sales talk. What does he say?
2. Instead of wringing the rooster's neck, the girls stuff him into a sack and take him to market to sell. What happens?
3. An old sorceress, who conjures spells to order and mixes potions, lives in the neighborhood. The girls pay her a visit with a request. What is the conversation?
4. The girls discover a dark room, with no windows, in the house. They hide the rooster in there hoping he will be confused. The chickens miss him and come looking for him thinking he is playing hide and seek. Play the game in the house as the chickens would!
5. Everytime the rooster crows, have a chorus recite along with him, "Cock-a-doodle-doo, there's no more sleep for you."
6. What can you remember about the time when you did something you thought was very smart, and it turned out to be very dumb?

Props to Use

Have actors wear signs identifying their characters. Post signs for any other information when needed to help the play.

= Bonnets, aprons, overalls, jeans for the girls
= A grey wig for the woman or powdered hair
= A red hat, knit cap or red tam for the rooster
= Fluffy red houseshoes for the rooster
= A big red sweater for the rooster
= Cushions for the girls in bed
= Buckets, baskets, boxes for feeding chickens, milking the cow and slopping the pigs

My Name _____

SHOWTIME SKILLS

THE NAME OF THE PLAY WAS _____
_____

CHARACTERS IN THE PLAY: ACTED BY:

_____   _____
_____   _____
_____   _____
_____   _____
_____   _____

• •

THE PLAY MADE ME FEEL _____
_____
_____

I LIKED IT BEST WHEN _____
_____
_____

MY FAVORITE CHARACTER WAS _____
_____
_____

I LIKED THIS CHARACTER BECAUSE _____
_____
_____

A DIFFERENT TITLE COULD BE _____
_____
_____

IF I COULD CHANGE THE ENDING, I WOULD _____
_____
_____

THE TRAVELLERS AND THE BEAR
A True Friend Is There, Even in Time of Trouble

THE TRAVELLERS AND THE BEAR

CAST OF CHARACTERS:

Simon
Simon's wife
Clyde
Bear

"I am leaving for a long journey into town this afternoon." The man whose name was Simon sat and drank his breakfast tea as he explained his plan for the day. "There is much business to attend to so please, good wife, do not expect my return until tomorrow noon!"

His wife, a jovial woman, said, "Let me pack you a lunch of your favorite things to eat." She pulled out a drawstring canvas bag and began filling it with victuals. While breaking big chunks of cheese and coarse bread, she attended to her task and talked out loud to herself listing all the snacks she included. "Here is the drumstick from a fat roasting chicken. I will give you nuts and sweetmeats, a strong white radish from the garden, and a bottle of cherry wine."

THE TRAVELLERS AND THE BEAR

Simon instructed his wife and said, "Increase the quantity of food you are packing by two, if you please, for it is my pleasure to be travelling with a friend this splendid day. It is a long trip and I will welcome his company."

Simon's pleasant wife turned to him, surprised. "A friend you say. Who is this friend?"

"A **good** friend," he replied.

"How is it you would have a **good** friend of whom I have never heard?" she wondered.

"I met him at a market fair some days ago," he answered impatienty. "We talked and were instantly in agreement about most everything. A most charming fellow! A most convivial person! A good friend, to be sure!"

"You have known this man for less than a week and already you speak of him as a dear and trusted friend. Have you taken leave of your senses?"

"My patience is wearing thin with your conversation, woman." He began to shout. "Why are you so suspicious? Why are you not willing to accept my judgment?"

THE TRAVELLERS AND THE BEAR

"Calm yourself," she patted his shoulder firmly to settle his temper. "In truth, I am glad you will have a travelling companion. It can sometimes be dangerous to travel alone, and I wish no harm to come to you, Simon. I will double the food in the sack for your friend."

He grumbled but responded to her kindness. "Please hurry. I promised to be at his door within the hour." They were silent as he readied himself to go. He picked up the sack of food and stood for a moment at the door waiting for her parting words because, in truth, he respected her good sense.

With great patience she offered her wisdom. "Real friends are people who have proven their loyalty over a period of time. They are there when you need them."

Before Simon knew it he had walked so fast he was at the door of his new friend. They greeted each other warmly as they set out for their walk to town. All the while Simon's friend Clyde hardly stopped talking. He was a robust fellow with a blustering style of speech which was a good bit louder than need be.

THE TRAVELLERS AND THE BEAR

"And what's for lunch?" inquired Clyde with enthusiasm. So pleased was he that he put his large arm around Simon's shoulder and carried on about their good fortune in having met one another. He talked excessively. "You are such a good fellow. I can tell we will be the very best of companions. What a pleasure to know such an agreeable man as yourself, Simon." He laughed heartily and pounded Simon on the back with each new declaration of friendship.

Except for Clyde's conversation, their trip up to this time was quiet and uneventful. Then--all at once--there was a thrashing and breaking of underbrush and a terrifying growl which forced their hearts into their mouths. What should appear through the separated thicket than the mean and threatening countenance of a surly brown bear.

Clyde, the newly acquired friend, was all energy and motion. He was surprisingly swift despite his girth. Without a thought for Simon, he scrambled up a tree like a coward in a fright. "It's everyone for himself!" he shouted hysterically.

THE TRAVELLERS AND THE BEAR

"Wait! Wait. Just wait for me a moment!" cried Simon, hobbling toward the tree, for he had turned his ankle in the sudden skirmish.

"Just give me a hand," he called desperately.

He broke for the tree but no hand was held out for his rescue. Resigned, Simon did the next best thing to save his hide. He threw himself on the ground and he lay there terrified but rigid, for he had heard, as many have, that bears will not bother with anything they think is dead. So Simon held his breath and pretended to be dead. He dared not breathe or turn a hair. He clamped his tongue against his teeth so that he would not cry out, for now the grizzly bear had approached him and had begun to investigate his spuriously lifeless form. The damp intrusive muzzle smelled Simon's face, explored his nose, probed his ears, and sniffed his hair. Carefully, carefully, the bear examined him. He turned Simon over with one huge paw and touched his chest, tearing at his shirt. Then, finally convinced that the man was dead, he shambled away, swaying slowly from side to side, grunting his disappointment.

THE TRAVELLERS AND THE BEAR

All the while Simon's erstwhile friend, concealed by the leaves and branches, watched from up high in the safety of the tree. When the bear had disappeared, Clyde shinnied down the trunk. "On my word I saw that bear whisper in your ear," he said curiously. "Make no mistake about it--I could see that he told you something. What was it that this wild creature would want to share with you?"

Simon stood and brushed the dirt from his clothes. He wiped his forehead with relief. His brow was furrowed and as his voice rose in anger he said, "There is no secret about his words to me--for it was only this--that with a friend like you I do not need an enemy. Only a scoundrel would leave a friend who is in so much danger."

The Point of the Story: A true friend is there, even in time of trouble.

Ideas to Dramatize or Discuss

1. Simon is looking through the morning paper at the breakfast table and reads a story about a roving bear. What is the conversation that follows between him and his wife?
2. When the travellers stop for lunch, they hang a large mirror on a nearby tree. The bear discovers the mirror and his own reflection. How does this affect him?
3. The bear seems friendly and starts to speak a strange language to the travellers. They try very hard to understand one another and carry on a confused conversation. Act out that conversation.
4. When Clyde climbs down the tree and the bear has departed, he thinks his friend Simon has really died of fright. What does he do? What story does he plan to tell the neighbors?
5. While the bear is sniffing around Simon, who is lying on the ground, a loud, flashy circus ringmaster comes crashing through the brush and tries to talk the bear into joining the good life of the circus.
6. The brave wife, worried about her husband, arrives on the scene with a shield and a prod. She talks to the bear, while keeping him under control, as they reach a peaceful agreement.
7. What kind of situation have you been in when you were grateful to be with a good friend?

Props to Use

Have actors wear signs identifying their characters. Post signs for any other information when needed to help the play.

- = Raincoats for the travellers
- = A fur hat, fur jacket, or fur coat for the bear
- = Head kerchief for the wife
- = Sack or lunch bucket for Simon and Clyde
- = Walking stick or umbrella for one traveller
- = A painted backdrop with signposts or a large map with directions to town

My Name _____

SHOWTIME SKILLS

THE NAME OF THE PLAY WAS _____
_____

CHARACTERS IN THE PLAY: ACTED BY:

_____   _____

_____   _____

_____   _____

_____   _____

_____   _____

• •

THE PLAY MADE ME FEEL _____
_____
_____

I LIKED IT BEST WHEN _____
_____
_____

MY FAVORITE CHARACTER WAS _____
_____

I LIKED THIS CHARACTER BECAUSE _____
_____
_____

A DIFFERENT TITLE COULD BE _____
_____

IF I COULD CHANGE THE ENDING, I WOULD _____
_____
_____

THE SICK LION
It Is Easier to Get into Trouble Than to Get Out

THE SICK LION

CAST OF CHARACTERS:

Lion
Lamb
A chorus of monkeys
Animal visitors
Fox

One day an old lion was seen walking very slowly down a dusty road. His age prevented him from hunting, but he had struck upon a cunning plan to make his prey come to him! A young, innocent lamb watched the poor lion as he wended his way to a nearby resting place.

"Where are you going and what is troubling you, oh great one?"

The lion, pretending he could hardly find his voice to reply, said weakly, "I am afraid that I am dying. Would you please be kind enough to tell all the animals you see today that the end of my life has come. In my last sad hours I will be waiting for them to make a final visit to me in my sickbed. It is my earnest wish, you see, to say good-bye to each and every one of them. All bad feelings are forgiven of my subjects!"

THE SICK LION

The innocent lamb put on a very sad face to show her sympathy for the lion and said, "You may depend upon me to do your bidding right away. But tell me, dear sire, is there anything else that I can do for you?"

"Oh yes," replied the huge beast shaking his mane feebly. "Please tell the creatures, too, that I will be reading my last will and testament."

"I am young and innocent and fail to understand the meaning of this," said the lamb.

The lion smiled a sly smile, "My will is a statement about what I will be leaving for each of my subjects after my death. I am sure they will want to hear of this."

"How good. How kind," said the tender lambkin to herself. "It is clear that the king of the beasts has often been misjudged. How wrong to think him unkind!"

The lamb, in her sweetness and concern, attended quickly to her task. She told the monkeys first and, as could be expected, they chattered the news all over the countryside.

THE SICK LION

In a chorus they proclaimed:

> "THE LION SITS INSIDE HIS CAVE
> HE FACES DEATH.
> HE IS SO BRAVE."

XXXXXXX

> "COME VISIT IF YOU CARE.
> CONSOLE HIM IF YOU DARE!"

XXXXXXX

The wee lamb said to the bull, "The lion dies. He sends his forgiveness for all old grudges."

The bull said to the mule, "The lion dies and gasps for breath. He wants to share his riches before passing."

The mule said to the goat, "Come say good-bye. The lion has such little time to live."

THE SICK LION

Once again, a chorus of monkeys were heard to chant:

"THE LION SITS INSIDE HIS CAVE
HE FACES DEATH.
HE IS SO BRAVE."

XXXXXXXX

"COME VISIT IF YOU CARE.
CONSOLE HIM IF YOU DARE!"

XXXXXXXX

In a chain of communication the news travelled like a fire in the forest until it reach-ed the fox. "This is indeed strange," she said to no one in particular, as she stroked her chin. "I saw him just the other day and, though he had a terrible cough, he was hardly at death's door! I must investigate this for myself." The fox who was as sly as foxes can be trotted to the scene but decided not to enter the cave immediately. Instead she hid behind a bush and watched the opening of the lion's den where hung a cheery sign which read, **WELCOME ONE AND ALL.**

THE SICK LION

The fox watched the guileless animals file in all day long to the lion's last resting place. They came alone. They came in pairs. Some of them even came bearing gifts for their sick monarch. Each of them entered the den but strangely, not a single one of them could be seen leaving.

"What have you brought for the King of the Beasts?"

"A gift most rare."

"I bring him news from afar."

"These flowers are for him."

"Some water from the spring."

"Regards from his oldest relatives."

"Secrets to please his fancy."

But still the fox waited. Soon, at the entrance of his lair, the great shaggy mane of the lion appeared. His eyes were bright and his voice was strong. The old rascal seemed powerful and well, as always.

THE SICK LION

Looking toward the fox he said imploringly, "Will you not come in, dear vixen, to say a last good-bye to your sick and ailing monarch?" The lion coughed weakly a few times, covering his mouth delicately with his paw.

"I should like so much to speak with you."

"Forgive me now your royal majesty," said the fox courteously, "but so many of your good subjects have entered your lair and none seem to exit. Surely, it must be crowded beyond the limits of that place." The fox bowed deeply and with great formality said, "I believe I will just stay outside in the sweetness of the open air. From the distance of this tree I shall send my respectful farewells, for I prefer not to go in if I see no way out."

The Point of the Story: It is easier to get into trouble than to get out.

79

Ideas to Dramatize or Discuss

1. Have a chorus of monkeys recite, "The lion sits inside his cave. He faces death. He is so brave." Use the chorus at whatever points in the play it would be most effective.
2. A town doctor is invited by the animals to make a house call to the lion in his den. What happens?
3. A laughing hyena talks to the animals about all the terrible things the lion has done to them. She wants to be their new ruler. She laughs a lot when she speaks.
4. A monkey brings the lion a gift box of bubble gum. What happens? Perform the lion's problems with the gum.
5. A wise old owl tries to smarten up the animals about what the lion is doing. He holds a scarey night meeting because he can only see in the dark. How do the animals behave at the meeting?
6. The animals are so sure their king is dying that they compose an obituary for him as he stands and listens. It ends with "REST IN PEACE." Write and read the obituary.
7. Never before have the animals been to a medicine show. One comes into town and the medicine man sells his homemade potion that will cure everything. What will the animals do with it?
8. Do you recall ever getting into trouble easily only to discover that it was very hard to get out? Can you talk about it?

Props to Use

Have actors wear signs identifying their characters. Post signs for any other information when needed to help the play.

= Red "medicine" with a spoon for the lion to use
= A big mop of hair for the lion's mane
= Mittens for the lion's paws
= Wrapped presents brought by the visiting animals
= A sheet draped over a table for the lion's lair
= Artificial flowers carried by the reluctant fox
= Eyebrow pencil, paste-on or yarn whiskers for the lion
= A make-believe thermometer for the lion's mouth
= A large bow for the fox

My Name _____

SHOWTIME SKILLS

THE NAME OF THE PLAY WAS _____
_____

CHARACTERS IN THE PLAY: ACTED BY:

_____   _____
_____   _____
_____   _____
_____   _____
_____   _____

• •

THE PLAY MADE ME FEEL _____
_____
_____

I LIKED IT BEST WHEN _____
_____
_____

MY FAVORITE CHARACTER WAS _____
_____
_____

I LIKED THIS CHARACTER BECAUSE _____
_____
_____

A DIFFERENT TITLE COULD BE _____
_____
_____

IF I COULD CHANGE THE ENDING, I WOULD _____
_____
_____

THE EAGLE, THE WILDCAT, AND THE SOW
Anyone Who Gossips to You Will Gossip About You

THE EAGLE, THE WILDCAT, AND THE SOW

CAST OF CHARACTERS:

Mrs. Eagle
Mrs. Wildcat
Mrs. Sow

Very high in the sky where the clouds floated elegantly in the blue, there flew a mother eagle. Like all eagles, she had eyes that could see animals and their movements on the ground as she soared majestically. In time she came upon an old oak tree which towered against the sky. It was tall and strong. The full branches, at the crown of the tree, reached up extending an invitation to the eagle, and she made her decision. Looking down she said, "Here is the ideal place for a nest on these stout limbs below. I will settle here, make a nest, lay my eggs, and hatch my young ones." The great sweep of her magnificent wings brought her to a graceful landing, and she settled into her new home.

THE EAGLE, THE WILDCAT, AND THE SOW

Sometime later a sow came walking by on light little feet. She stopped at the old tree and saw the eagle nesting at the top. Looking up as high as she could, she called out to the eagle.

"Dear Madam, it is not my wish to disturb you, but I am looking for a place to raise my little piglets. Since you are the only occupant about--may I ask if you would kindly share this tree with me?"

Thinking the sow to be a pleasant enough creature and surely no threat to her family she said, "Be my guest. There is no reason why we cannot live peacefully together. It is only the top of the tree that we need."

An appreciative smile creased the face of the sow. "My home will be down below among the roots. I will dig a comfortable burrow with my snout and my front feet. And there in the cool of the earth I will care for my darling babies. Thank you, Mrs. Eagle."

"You're welcome, Mrs. Sow."

THE EAGLE, THE WILDCAT, AND THE SOW

The two families lived very happily together though afar. They said good morning and good evening, one from the very top of the oak, the other from the very bottom. They could be seen attending to their own affairs--the pig rooting, the eagle soaring.

At a later time a striped mother wildcat was seen walking by ever so softly, ever so gracefully. Looking down at the roots she saw the sow.

"How goes it with you, Madam Eagle? May I move into your tree with my little cats?"

"It is fine with me. Ask the other tenant of the tree if she feels kindly disposed toward more occupants."

"How goes it with you, Madam Sow? May I move in with my little cats?"

"You are most welcome to the tree, for we are cordial friends, the eagle and I. There is room enough for all of us. Where will your house be?" asked the sow.

THE EAGLE, THE WILDCAT, AND THE SOW

"My den will be in the hollow trunk of this oak. I can move in on this very day."

Soon, any passerby could see little pink piglets with twisted little tails at the roots of the host tree, bald little eagle heads at the top, and whiskers and piercing little eyes hiding in the hollow of the tree. Life was serene, and one would never guess there was any trouble in the world.

The mothers were seldom idle. They came and went in search of life's necessities, cared for their homes and lived in harmony until one sad day the wildcat--who for reasons of her own was given to nasty ways--began to gossip. "How nice it would be to have this tree all to myself. The trouble will not be hard to start," she said, as she planned that day to do mischief.

First, she went to the mother sow. "Mrs. Sow, I must tell you that I heard Mrs. Eagle promising her babies a delicious meal of pork, one day quite soon. I heard it with my own ears this very week."

THE EAGLE, THE WILDCAT, AND THE SOW

"My word. Oh heavens above," the sow said as she fell apart with dismay, for she was cruelly scared. "This means I cannot go out in search of food for my little shoats. What shall I do? Are you certain this is true?" she moaned.

"Would I mislead you just for the sport of it?" asked the wildcat with feigned innocence.

And so the poor pig did not move from her home. She and her family grew hungry, for she kept a constant vigil to guard the safety of her young.

Now it was time for the wildcat to try her vicious game with the eagle. The cat whispered to the eagle who, one busy day, was away from the tree on domestic business. "Far be it for me to gossip, Mrs. Eagle, but perhaps you have not noticed how Mrs. Sow spends her time. She digs and prods and pokes out the roots of this poor old tree so vigorously that one day she will surely loosen it from the ground and cause it to tumble down, smashing our home to slivers and kindling wood. Then where will we all be without a place to live?"

THE EAGLE, THE WILDCAT, AND THE SOW

The eagle was quieter in her distress than the pig had been, for she was a regal bird. She was, nonetheless, concerned. "I will keep a cautionary watch on what is going on down below at the base of this tree. If Mrs. Sow's natural habits cause my home to crash to the ground, I must be ready for such a circumstance."

The eagle did not leave her nest. Only the wildcat went out at night, which was her natural time to hunt and forage for food for her babies. But for the other two mothers, the consequence of the gossip was that they spent their days in fright and their nights in wakefulness, for now they distrusted each other.

This kind of life could not go on. Some glimmer of suspicion told Mrs. Eagle that all was not well. She no longer saw Mrs. Sow happily attending to her chores. Surely, Mrs. Sow had nothing to be frightened of. With great dignity the curious eagle flew down to the pig's house to validate the truth. She said to Mrs. Sow straightway, "You must leave the tree for the good of us all! The wildcat told me this about you."

THE EAGLE, THE WILDCAT, AND THE SOW

"But the cat told me that about you!" the pig replied.

"But the cat told me this about you!" the eagle rejoined.

"And the cat told me the other thing!" the pig responded.

Between this and that and the other thing, the two mothers arrived at the truth. The gossip's stories had made them distrust each other, and they had almost starved to death besides. How could they have been so foolish to believe such nasty tales? It was a hard lesson to learn, but they were sure never to forget it.

The pig shook her head seriously. "No one is safe from the wagging of a malicious tongue."

"If a gossip comes to you with a story about someone, you may be sure you will be the next on the list to be talked about," said the eagle.

THE EAGLE, THE WILDCAT, AND THE SOW

They conferred with one another and quickly hit upon a direct approach to confront the troublemaking wildcat. They were severe as they faced her. They repeated her lies and stories, which she could not deny, and hastened to inform her that she was banished from the tree home forever. The wildcat retired from the forest and was consumed with shame for her breach of decency.

The two remaining mothers were heard to say,

"Thank you, Mrs. Eagle."

You're welcome, Mrs. Sow."

The Point of the Story: Anyone who gossips to you will gossip about you.

Ideas to Dramatize or Discuss

1. Give the tree a speaking part. How does it feel about its tenants?
2. A builder comes to tell the tenants that all the trees in the area must be cut down for a construction project. What will the tenants say? What will the builder say? Do they argue?
3. A little piglet asks Mrs. Eagle to give him flying lessons. She puts him into her nest way up high. How does he feel and act when he looks down?
4. The wildcat sends a letter to the eagle and the sow. It is delivered by a mail carrier. How does the carrier find them as she tries to make her delivery in the forest? Whom does she talk to?
5. A salesperson wants to use the animals' names for advertising. All of the creatures must give their permission. What products does the salesperson want to sell with their names attached? (Examples might be: Eagle eyeglasses, Wildcat running shoes, and Piggy banks.) Perform the role of the salesperson and be convincing.
6. Choose a narrator to give some interesting scientific information about the life and habits of the eagle, the wildcat, and the sow. The creatures may demonstrate their characteristics as they are described by the narrator.
7. What fourth creature might come to live in the tree with the others? How might this change everything for all of them?
8. Create a gossip experience for the entire class. With everyone in a circle, whisper a message into the ear of the first person, who whispers the same message into the ear of his/her neighbor. When the message has arrived at the last person, ask to hear it out loud. Is the information the same or has it changed? What does this tell you about gossip?

Props to Use

Have actors wear signs identifying their characters. Post signs for any other information when needed to help the play.

= Eyebrow pencil whiskers for the wildcat
= Goggles for the wildcat
= A pink shirt with stuffing in it for the pig
= A construction paper headband with construction paper feathers for the eagle
= White eye makeup in circles around the eyes for the eagle
= A green rug for a patch of forest
= High heeled shoes for the pig

My Name _____

SHOWTIME SKILLS

THE NAME OF THE PLAY WAS _____
_____

CHARACTERS IN THE PLAY: ACTED BY:

_____   _____

_____   _____

_____   _____

_____   _____

_____   _____

• •

THE PLAY MADE ME FEEL _____
_____
_____

I LIKED IT BEST WHEN _____
_____

MY FAVORITE CHARACTER WAS _____
_____
_____

I LIKED THIS CHARACTER BECAUSE _____
_____
_____

A DIFFERENT TITLE COULD BE _____
_____
_____

IF I COULD CHANGE THE ENDING, I WOULD _____
_____
_____

THE NURSEMAID AND THE WOLF
Don't Believe Everything You Hear

THE NURSEMAID AND THE WOLF

CAST OF CHARACTERS:

Crow
Wolf
Nursemaid
Child

A shining blue-black crow was circling a clearing near a village. As she flew she was being carefully observed by a wolf who looked dreadfully bedraggled and bone thin. The crow landed on a branch in the tree, and as if to divert the wolf's intent, the clever bird engaged the scraggly creature in conversation.

"What are you doing such a distance from home?" she asked the wolf, settling her own burnished feathers. "I have surely seen you looking better!"

The wolf responded, "How pleased I am for your kind interest, madam. Frankly my wanderings have taken me this far, for I am famished to the point of pain."

As he spoke, the whiteness of his sharp teeth were strong in evidence to the crow. Hoping to discourage any notions the wolf might have with regard to herself, the crow offered the following help:

"During my flight, on this very day, I have seen many fine things to eat in the town of which I am a native. Come, let me take you there."

"I shall not refuse," said the wolf, "for it has been more time than I can measure since my last meal. I am willing to chance any adventure. Will you show me the way?"

In the fullness of her generosity, the crow gave directions. "Keep looking in the air as I take off. My course will take you north into town where you will surely sup tonight."

THE NURSEMAID AND THE WOLF

When he arrived in the bustling little town, the wolf was alert for any possibilities of nourishment. A short time later, chance took him to the open window of the cottage where he overheard the strident voice of a nursemaid scolding a young child.

"You will do as you are told, you naughty child. No more sweets for you before your evening meal. You have wasted your appetite once again gorging yourself on forbidden foods."

The wolf paused. He stood as a statue, in his tracks, to listen more closely to the nature of this argument, for the very talk of supper and forbidden things to eat filled his mind with happy thoughts. His muzzle quivered, saliva flowed in his mouth, and his tongue lolled over his teeth.

"Now let us try again to eat our dinner," coaxed the nursemaid. "I will tie your bib under your chin. Don't be in such a pout when I talk to you. Wipe that defiant look from your face. It is unbecoming for a child as young as you." Her voice was shrill as she was trying earnestly to win the contest.

With his curiosity greatly aroused, the wolf looked into the window which was just low enough for his projecting jaws to rest upon. He saw the saucy scamp, with his round pink face and his little well-fed belly. The nasty child was turning his face away and refusing spoon after spoon of tasty food, as he retorted, "You cannot keep me from the jams and jellies. You cannot keep me from the honey-butter in the pantry or from the plum pudding or the caramel sauce." The baby wailed like an uncivilized little whelp!

THE NURSEMAID AND THE WOLF

At this, the wolf grew fainter with deprivation. His ears perked up. His stomach began to growl. He swooned with jealousy of the privileged life of this ungrateful child.

"If I hear more to tempt my palate, I do not know what I shall do," the wolf whimpered. He pressed his ear closer to the window so as not to miss a word, so lustful was his hunger.

"Don't push me, you ill-mannered imp," the nurse said. "Your mother and father will hear of this." She smacked his hands in a sharp rebuke for his discourtesy. The baby tried to fend off blows with his sticky hands. It was very obvious, even to the casual observer, that the two of them were most practiced in this kind of battle.

Unaware of the wild creature outside his window, from whom he had much more to fear than from his nursemaid, the boy cried out, "The trifle you prepared for company shall be mine with all the almond custard and chocolate and lady fingers layered with jelly in the bowl. It is mine, it is mine!"

THE NURSEMAID AND THE WOLF

The wolf was hypnotized by this menu. No longer was he able to support his own weight. He wished dearly to jump through the window but feared for the dogs which were likely kept in the household.

"Woe is me. Woe is me. I shall not survive this torture too much longer." But fate, it would seem, turned in the wolf's favor. For what should he hear but an astonishing statement from the nursemaid!

"Insolent boy. I shall clamp my hand over your mouth, and you will cease this impudent behavior!"

She did precisely that, but the recital did not stop. Sounds of the child's protests were muffled under her hand. And then the wolf heard it. He heard her incredible promise.

"IF YOU DO NOT CEASE THIS BEHAVIOR I SHALL PICK YOU UP BODILY AND THROW YOU OUT THE WINDOW TO ANY WOLF WHO HAPPENS TO BE PASSING BY! Plump little children with rounded cheeks and pretty dimples are the favorite dish of hungry wolves. Some wolf shall thank me greatly to have you for his supper."

THE NURSEMAID AND THE WOLF

"On my soul," thought the wolf, "does she really know that I am here?"

"Wa, wa, wa," the child screamed. "Wa, wa, wa," he continued in terror. "Wa, wa, wa," was all the wolf heard.

"Heaven smiles on me this glorious day. I must prepare myself for a superb supper," said the wolf rubbing his paws together. "I have heard from the nurse's very own lips that she will toss my supper out the window."

With renewed patience he sat and waited to catch the child whom the nurse had promised to toss out the window. He sat and he sat. He waited very long. Still there was nothing to feed his raging appetite.

Darkness wrapped the entire village in its mantle. The clock struck a late hour and bedtime moved into the household. All at once, a low crooning wafted through the window, as the nurse's voice sang.

THE NURSEMAID AND THE WOLF

"I forgive you as I always do. Sleep my sweet one. Sleep my precious. Rest my little lamb. There will be no wolf for you, dear heart. Instead, we send the dogs out to get the wolf."

It was certain now that there was no good dinner to be had here. The wolf skulked away, sorely disappointed.

"There is something worse than hunger for me to worry about. I hear the barking of the dogs in the house. I had better turn tail and escape quickly, for my life is in danger. What a fool I have been to have taken the nursemaid's silly promise seriously. Too bad for me--but people do not always mean what they say."

The Point of the Story: Don't believe everything you hear.

Ideas to Dramatize or Discuss

1. The wolf, listening at the window, becomes angry with the behavior of the child. The wolf forgets that he is hiding and begins to shout at the child for his bad manners.

2. One of the dogs from the house comes out and meets the wolf who tries to pretend he is a dog, too. The dog is suspicious and asks a lot of questions. How does the wolf answer?

3. Remembering the story of "The Three Little Pigs," the wolf decides to use the same routine with the nursemaid. He says, "I'll huff and I'll puff and I'll blow the house in." How does the nursemaid respond?

4. The wolf decides to sing and dance for his supper. How does he perform? How do the neighbors act toward a dancing wolf?

5. Tired and hungry, the wolf lies down and dreams he is in a restaurant, reading a menu and giving his order to a person who is the nursemaid. What does he order? Perform this scene.

6. A werewolf is a man who becomes transformed into a wolf at night. This unfortunate person meets the wolf and tells him the sad story of his miserable life. How does the wolf act toward the man?

7. Did you ever decide that it was better not to believe everything you hear? Can you talk about it?

Props to Use

Have actors wear signs identifying their characters. Post signs for any other information when needed to help the play.

= A brown or black jacket for the wolf
= Shabby gloves for the wolf
= White cap for the nursemaid
= White dress for the nursemaid
= Bib for the child
= Bowl and spoon to feed the child
= A large cardboard window or a puppet stage as a window for the nurse and child
= A sign that says "People Do Not Always Mean What They Say"

My Name _____

SHOWTIME SKILLS

THE NAME OF THE PLAY WAS _____

_____

CHARACTERS IN THE PLAY: ACTED BY:

_____   _____

_____   _____

_____   _____

_____   _____

· ·

THE PLAY MADE ME FEEL _____

_____

_____

I LIKED IT BEST WHEN _____

_____

_____

MY FAVORITE CHARACTER WAS _____

_____

_____

I LIKED THIS CHARACTER BECAUSE _____

_____

_____

A DIFFERENT TITLE COULD BE _____

_____

_____

IF I COULD CHANGE THE ENDING, I WOULD _____

_____

_____

THE FARMER AND HIS CROWDED HOUSE
No Matter How Bad Things Seem, They Can Always Be Worse

THE FARMER AND HIS CROWDED HOUSE

CAST OF CHARACTERS:

Farmer
Wife
Farmer's children
Scholar
Farm animals

A farmer, who was a hardworking simple man, lived in a crude, modest home about which he had no complaints. When the farmer married and his family grew, his little home was hardly large enough for everyone. The true conditions in this cramped little household could best be judged by conversation shared by the children and overheard all through the day and night!

"You're eating from my bowl."

"I'm sorry. I thought it was my own."

"You sit too close. You're sitting on my lap."

"Our chairs are squeezed too close, I fear."

"Whose foot is in my shoe?"

"Whose else, but mine!"

"I cannot sleep for elbows in my ribs."

"You're standing on my toes."

"But someone stands on mine."

"Who wipes my nose as if it were his own?"

"Your arm is in my sleeve."

It was inevitable that one day the farmer's wife, who worked as hard as he, met him at the door upon his return from the fields. She was harried, one could see. "Good husband, our family grows larger and our home grows smaller with each passing day. Is there no way we can find a remedy for this problem?"

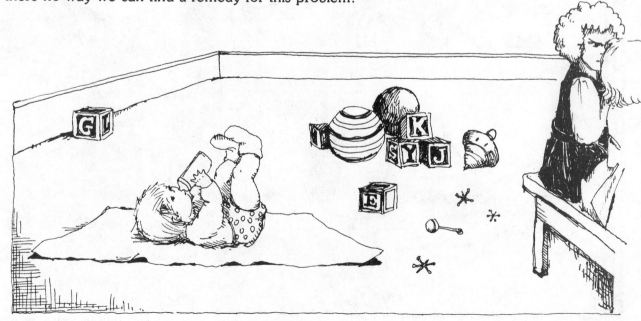

106

THE FARMER AND HIS CROWDED HOUSE

Sadly he reminded her, "There is barely enough money to take care of our daily needs, as it is. I cannot make our home any larger."

They both fell silent as they considered this problem together, for they were a kindly couple who enjoyed a mutual affection. They were most careful of one another's feelings. The wife wore a worried expression; the farmer cupped his chin in his hand and occasionally gave a sigh of discouragement.

"An idea just came to me," the wife brightened. "Why don't you venture to the house of the scholar, who is among the most learned of people. Perhaps she can help us!"

Dutifully he went to ask this favor of the scholar. "Since you are so wise in matters of learning, I wish to ask if you are as wise in the business of life." The farmer then gave a report of the calamitous state of affairs in his crowded house and described the burden of his problem.

The aged scholar listened attentively. She stroked her cheek and nodded her head, in the way of wise people. "Hm, hm," she said. "Hm. I will help you if I can, but after I deliver my opinion, you must promise faithfully to do precisely as I advise."

"I do. I do. I shall do just as you instruct."

THE FARMER AND HIS CROWDED HOUSE

The scholar fell silent for awhile. She examined the problem critically in her mind. She deliberated long and profoundly and then--and only then did she have a solution for the farmer.

"Go home and take the cow into your house the moment you arrive."

"What madness is this?" asked the distraught farmer.

"Do as you are told!" the scholar pointed towards the door.

The consternation that met the cow's arrival in the little house can hardly be described. The children bumped and trod on one another as before, but now the cow's tail and bovine body were in the way!

"I am eating Flossie's tail in my soup!"

"She moos in my ear so that I cannot hear."

"Her hind quarters push me into the fireplace."

"What strange solution is this to our problem?" whined the farmer's wife. "You must go back and talk to the wise woman once again."

They lived this way for a short time and soon the farmer yielded to his wife's demands.

"Our misery increases," the farmer explained to the scholar. "Please tell me what to do."

THE FARMER AND HIS CROWDED HOUSE

"Listen carefully, simple fellow! Go home and take in the goat and the pig." The farmer was struck dumb with this advice. He hesitated to go home, but the scholar pointed toward the door and shouted, "Go."

The farmer was frightened to tell his wife, but faithfully entered the house with the goat and the pig.

"The goat eats the straw from the mattress, Mother dear."

"I have slipped in the dirt from the pig, Father dear."

And so the children and the farmer and his wife and the cow and the goat and the pig shared the indignity of their crowded domestic life.

The wife was indignant. "Again, again. You must go again to see this person of wisdom who visits such disaster on our family."

Caught between his wife's temper and the wise woman's madness, he left, but only to soothe her anger, for he had long ago given up. With dread, the farmer entered the wise woman's house, once again. "Our lives are no better than those of the lowly beasts of the field. Indeed the animals are now living better than we are, and in our very own house."

"Go home and take in the horse!" And before the poor farmer could find his voice to protest, the wise woman ordered him to stuff in the chickens as well.

109

THE FARMER AND HIS CROWDED HOUSE

By now, life for the family had become a nightmare. There was no room to sit, to stand, to sleep, to eat, to breathe. And with the overwhelming sounds of the animals, the family could no longer hear each other speak. The air was thick with barnyard smells, and the feathers flew all around and around.

"Enough, enough, this is enough," shrieked the wife, as she pushed her husband out the door for one last visit to the scholar. He left in despair.

"Good morrow, country fellow, I have been waiting for you," said the scholar brightly.

The farmer responded with a weariness that seeped from his very bones, for he had not slept in a dog's age. "We have reached the limits of our endurance," he sighed. "I come now only to tell you that our sanity is all but destroyed."

"Go home then, this very minute as quickly as you can. Push out the cow, kick out the horse, force out the pig, slap out the goat, and chase out the chickens with a broom. Open your doors and windows wide and let the welcome air inside."

THE FARMER AND HIS CROWDED HOUSE

The farmer ran full speed ahead to carry the joyous news. Barely had he reached his door when he commenced to holler, "Out, out, the animals all go out. The wise woman says they must all go out."

Everyone helped, as they scampered and shouted and forced the surprised animals out of the bursting little house.

"Open the doors--open the windows--welcome the sun and the air once again." Then there fell upon each and every one of them a most astonishing silence. No one spoke, nor did they move--as they discovered such space, such room, such glorious expanse of floor in their little house. They rejoiced with the amplitude of their precious house just newly found. They jumped, they ran, they twirled! There was never again a complaint about space.

One last time, the farmer knocked upon the door of the scholar and handed her the gift of a nice plump roasting chicken. The farmer thanked the wise woman who smiled a knowing smile.

The Point of the Story: No matter how bad things seem, they can always be worse.

Ideas to Dramatize or Discuss

1. The children suggest that their parents charge admission to tourists to come and see "the most crowded house in the world." The children go to town and pass out handbills to attract customers and talk up their strange and wonderful sideshow.
2. A kindly neighbor overhears the farmer sharing his problem with the wise woman, but thinks the advice given is crazy. The neighbor talks with the farmer about the problem. What is his different solution?
3. The wife decides that she must find a job in town to earn extra money. What job does she apply for? Perform a job interview with the mother.
4. The children cultivate vegetables in their own little garden. They set up a roadside produce stand to earn money for their family. They perform a singing commercial at the side of the road to attract customers. Compose and sing that song.
5. Grandma and Grandpa set up a tutoring service and visit other houses to help the farmers and their children learn how to read and write. They will accept money or goods for their services. Act out a tutoring session.
6. Can you think of a time when you realized that no matter how bad things were, they could always be worse? What was the situation?

Props to Use

Have actors wear signs identifying their characters. Post signs for any other information when needed to help the play.

= Overalls, blue jeans, kerchiefs for the farmer and his family
= A rake or hoe or garden tools or baskets for the farm
= A watering can
= Balls, jump ropes, toys for the children
= A large painted sign that says "Home Sweet Home"
= Soup bowls and plastic tumblers for the table
= A shawl for the wise woman scholar

My Name _____

SHOWTIME SKILLS

THE NAME OF THE PLAY WAS _____
_____

CHARACTERS IN THE PLAY: ACTED BY:

_____   _____
_____   _____
_____   _____
_____   _____
_____   _____

* *

THE PLAY MADE ME FEEL _____
_____
_____

I LIKED IT BEST WHEN _____
_____
_____

MY FAVORITE CHARACTER WAS _____
_____

I LIKED THIS CHARACTER BECAUSE _____
_____
_____

A DIFFERENT TITLE COULD BE _____
_____
_____

IF I COULD CHANGE THE ENDING, I WOULD _____
_____
_____

THE MICE IN COUNCIL
Many People Have Good Ideas, But Few Act Upon Them

THE MICE IN COUNCIL

CAST OF CHARACTERS:

Jasper, the cat
Young mouse
Old mouse
Other mice

There once was a house cat who was of most undistinguished bearing and color. He was striped in odd directions and belonged to a very common breed of felines. He lived in a house inhabited by many families of mice. He prospered, in time, for services rendered to the human family with whom he enjoyed his room and board. As might be expected, he was known in these parts as Jasper, the fat cat. Over the years his reign of terror had become legend among the little mice.

At the very moment of this telling, Jasper was at yet another opening at the woodwork, glaring into the hole, intimidating the mouse population. He called in, "Come hither, my darlings and let me introduce myself to the youngest among your issue. Have you told your little ones how they must be guarded on their way to anywhere in this house? Come, come, sweethearts. Where are you?" This last question was delivered as musically as if it were a song.

THE MICE IN COUNCIL

Now the old mice made it a practice never to dignify Jasper's taunts with any replies. They did not want to encourage his arrogance. A young mouse, just coming into his maturity, opened his mouth to reply. But he was shushed by one of his elders, who shook a stern finger under his nose.

"Try to understand, young one. We do not want to engage the cat in any conversation. We do not want him to guess at our strength and numbers, for he has too much control as it is. He is never quite sure where we have set up housekeeping. If we rise to his bait and answer, he will be at every mouse's front door just from the location of our voices. He will have charted our population."

The young mouse only swaggered and assumed an expression of contempt in response, but he did not open his mouth to the older mouse again that day.

THE MICE IN COUNCIL

Jasper's voice was heard again. He flouted his power. "Why haven't I seen you lately, scurrying about the kitchen floor in search of crumbs or scouting in my mistress' pantry for bits of cheese? Could it be that the whole lot of you are humbled by my presence?"

Once again there was not a word spoken by the mice. Instead, they huddled in large groups, the better to hear the cat as he poked his nose into the very places where he guessed they hid. They moved in clusters at every booming threat of his voice, shoving each other and whispering caution as they stood. Jasper's voice was heard through the walls, under the steps, and beneath the cellar door.

THE MICE IN COUNCIL

As often happens, the young mice were in disagreement with their elders.

"Why do we have to live like this in such a state of fear?"

"Why can't our older members be smarter and more courageous than they are?"

"This is humiliating for a tribe of mice as distinguished as we!"

There were the rumblings of rebellion, and the young mice made signs and placards which they posted and carried all over. They marched and they made speeches to enlist others in their cause.

"Come to a meeting for the future of mousedom."

"Look to the young for a fresh start."

"Don't be trapped by the old ways."

"Nip this cat in the bud."

THE MICE IN COUNCIL

An emergency assembly was called by the young mice. Everyone from all over the vast house attended. They were prepared to listen to anyone.

The chairperson pounded her gavel. Bang, Bang, Bang! This meeting is now in session! Suggestions flew. But none captured the hearts of the council.

"Why don't we swarm and attack?"

"Turn the family against him."

"Find a dog to hound him."

Just then a young mouse full of self-importance rose and waited for the silence and attention of the Council. "It is my opinion that all of you must now put your confidence in me." His chest swelled. There was a long pause. "We must hang a bell from the neck of the cat so that we will know where he is at all times. The bell will always give us warning when he is near. Never again will we have to worry about our safety."

THE MICE IN COUNCIL

He stood waiting for the praise that he felt was due him. What a golden moment, he thought!

The crowd rose, whistling and applauding the wisdom of the young mouse. The chairperson banged her gavel but could not bring order, when finally, a very old and respected mouse who stood at the back of the crowd asked a devilish question.

"This is indeed an impressive and interesting suggestion. But who, pray tell, will volunteer to tie the bell around the cat's neck?"

The council fell suddenly silent--for none among them would volunteer to bell the cat.

The Point of the Story: Many people have good ideas, but few act upon them.

Ideas to Dramatize or Discuss

1. The teacher in the Mouse Elementary School tells the children about how to make a cat's cradle. What does he tell them about this game? Demonstrate his instructions to the mouse students.
2. A young mouse describes to some friends the experience of seeing the cat for the very first time. From the mouse's point of view, how did the cat look and move? Act out these impressions.
3. While the cat is asleep, the mice set a trap with a network of heavy wool yarn. How do they do it? What happens when the cat awakens? Act out the situation.
4. Using appropriate facial expressions, demonstrate the different emotions which occur in this story. Be either the cat or a mouse. How would you look if:
   - You are the cat threatening the mice
   - You are a frightened mouse listening to the cat
   - You are a tough mouse determined to fight back
   - You are the young mouse who just suggested belling the cat
   - You are the old wise mouse who just asked who would do the belling
5. In the street, the mice find a scrappy dog who is friendly to mice. They try to convince him that their house is a good place for him. What can they say to make the house sound interesting to the dog?
6. Some brave mice really do try to bell the cat. What happens?
7. Have you ever had a great idea for something? What was it?

Props to Use

Have actors wear signs identifying their characters. Post signs for any other information when needed to help the play.

= Wool stocking caps for all the mice
= A big silk bow for the cat
= A bell for the young mouse to show at the meeting
= A gavel for the chairperson of the mouse meeting
= Big furry bedroom slippers for the cat's feet
= A large mustache of yarn for the cat
= Classroom furniture to hide behind
= A backdrop of a giant cat's face with huge eyes

My Name _____

SHOWTIME SKILLS

THE NAME OF THE PLAY WAS _____

_____

CHARACTERS IN THE PLAY: ACTED BY:

_____   _____

_____   _____

_____   _____

_____   _____

• •

THE PLAY MADE ME FEEL _____

_____

I LIKED IT BEST WHEN _____

_____

MY FAVORITE CHARACTER WAS _____

_____

I LIKED THIS CHARACTER BECAUSE _____

_____

A DIFFERENT TITLE COULD BE _____

_____

IF I COULD CHANGE THE ENDING, I WOULD _____

_____

THE MILKMAID AND HER BUCKET
Don't Count Your Chickens Before They Hatch

THE MILKMAID AND HER BUCKET

CAST OF CHARACTERS:

Becky the milkmaid
Grandparents
Man
Woman
Boys at the fair

It was in the nature of a certain pleasant young milkmaid to daydream. Her name was Becky. She would do her work, fetch and carry, milk the cows, but all the while she went about her daily tasks, she would have a continuing fantasy. Her head was always full of plans, and she thought about many things that could happen that would make her life different or exciting. Her dreams were neither large, nor truly grand but only modest in size. She would say, for example, "If I baked the best cherry pie in the county, I would take it to the fair. The judges would say, 'Ooh and Ahh,' and then they would award me a blue ribbon which I would wear on my weskit for all to see."

Becky would invent so many plans for the future that they seemed quite real to her. Always lost in a new scheme, she would talk to herself and dramatize the little adventures which resided in her head.

"What is our precious Becky thinking about now?" her grandfather inquired of her grandmother, for Becky lived with them and they loved her dearly.

"It is just another of her reveries. I am afraid they seem very real to her, but if it gives her pleasure, it is a harmless pastime."

With the affection that grandparents feel for their grandchildren, the old couple called to their dear little milkmaid one clear and balmy morning.

"We are poor, Becky, and cannot give you much, but we have decided that today, when you milk the cow, you may take the milk to market and keep the money for your very own!"

THE MILKMAID AND HER BUCKET

The tender maid clapped her hands and jumped with joy. She felt such gratitude to her grandparents. Immediately, Becky conjured up some possibilities. "I will start with the milk money and then earn more and more. In this way I will make my dreams come true!"

With a cautionary note in his voice, Grandfather said, "Be calm, dear child. To expect that all your fancies will come true because of a bucket of milk seems too much to expect."

Becky milked the cow and watched each drop add to the precious milk she would carry to the market. She picked up the bucket with special care and headed out toward town. Almost as soon as she made her way on the country road, she was adrift in thought. Becky daydreamed of all the good that would come from the gift of the milk.

"I could separate the milk from the cream and churn the cream into rich, sweet-tasting butter. A man might come along and ask to buy my butter." She could see the man in her imagination as if he were really there.

127

THE MILKMAID AND HER BUCKET

"May I buy your delicious butter," the man might ask. "It is positively the very best I have seen. Any price you set will be fine with me. I will be pleased to pay you. Then I will take it home and give it to my wife who will spread it on fresh wheat bread from the oven. The butter will melt into all the pores of the bread, and my wife will serve it to our hungry children."

The imaginary man disappeared and now Becky made more plans. She clutched the milk bucket tightly.

"The money the gentleman would pay me for the butter could buy me some eggs!" she smiled as she carried the bucket of milk. Then, as one would expect, she thought about meeting a kind lady carrying a covered basket.

"I will ask the lady what she carries and she will say: 'This is a very special basket of my very finest setting eggs.' "

Becky went through the make-believe motions of a transaction. Had anyone seen her they would have thought her very strange, as she paid invisible money for invisible eggs to a woman who was not there.

THE MILKMAID AND HER BUCKET

Becky would place the eggs gently on the soft grass, and then she would sit watching expectantly, cupping her chin in her hands. As if by magic the eggs would hatch, one by one, and each feathered yellow chick would pick its way out of its fragile shell. The downy little heads would pop out, curious and new to the world.

Out loud she said, "I can almost see them now chirping and scratching around my feet. And from all of them I will make my fortune. I will gather them together and sell them for a handsome price to the very next person who comes down the road."

She walked along more hurriedly now, for she was becoming more excited with her fancy. She clutched her milk bucket and said, "With all the money from the chicks I will buy a beautiful dress of lace and lovely colored ribbons. Then I will be ready for the fair. Oh, how I yearn to go to the fair. I will look prettier than I have ever looked before. When I arrive the boys will gather 'round. I can hear them now."

THE MILKMAID AND HER BUCKET

"Dance with me," the first boy will say.

"No, dance with me," the second boy will say.

"It is me you must dance with!" the third boy will say.

But Becky thought she would be haughty and would tell them to go away. At that crucial moment, in her play acting, she completely forgot that she was carrying a bucket of milk. Can you believe that she shrugged her shoulders, put her hands on her hips, and let go of her precious bucket! The milk splattered to the ground before she realized what she had done. It soaked into the dirt. It was irretrievably gone. And with it ended all her dreams.

There would be no butter to sell from the cream. There would be no setting eggs to buy. There would be no little chicks hatching out of eggs. And there certainly would be no money to buy a dress with ribbons for the fair.

THE MILKMAID AND HER BUCKET

With tears of grief, Becky ran all the way home to tell her beloved grandparents what had happened. They listened patiently and soothed her. "There, there," they said. "It will be all right." They patted her hair and held her close. "Everything we plan does not always come true." Becky grew quieter then, as her grandparents consoled her. "Don't weep, poor child, for there is no sense in crying over spilled milk."

The Point of the Story: Don't count your chickens before they hatch.

Ideas to Dramatize or Discuss

1. Pretend that Becky used a covered milk can instead of an open bucket to carry the milk to market. If she got the milk there safely, does that mean that all the rest of her dreams would come true? What could happen?

2. Set up game booths and food booths at the fair. Have the vendors call out their wares to attract customers: "Four tosses for a quarter," "Get all the sweet corn you can eat," "Candy floss, candy floss," "Let's guess your weight for a prize."

3. The milkmaid decides to buy real eggs. She puts them under a setting hen which she borrows from a farmer. Every day she visits the hen sitting on the eggs but nothing hatches. She scolds the hen for not doing her job. The hen scolds back. Something is the matter, but whom will Becky ask for an explanation? (Note: only fertilized eggs will hatch.)

4. Becky makes a trip to the fair, because it is fun to go there. She enters a pie-eating contest though she is not sure what it is all about. What happens?

5. Some of the neighboring farm children have never been to the fair or the marketplace. Becky tries to describe the good times and wonderful things that happen on such a trip. What does she tell them and what questions do they want her to answer?

6. A very special boy hears about Becky's sadness over the spilled milk. He gives her some beans which he tells her are magic. What happens then? What does he promise?

7. Did you ever count your chickens before they hatched? When did you plan seriously on something which didn't happen at all?

Props to Use

Have actors wear signs identifying their characters. Post signs for any other information when needed to help the play.

= A bucket for the milk
= A basket and a cardboard carton for eggs
= Fake eggs made from white paper
= A big apron for the milkmaid
= Hats and ties for the boys at the fair
= Suspenders for Grandpa
= Hair ribbons, flowers for the fair
= A hairnet or head kerchief for Grandma
= A background painting of little chicks hatching out of eggs

My Name _____

SHOWTIME SKILLS

THE NAME OF THE PLAY WAS _____
_____

CHARACTERS IN THE PLAY: ACTED BY:

_____   _____

_____   _____

_____   _____

_____   _____

_____   _____

* *

THE PLAY MADE ME FEEL _____
_____
_____

I LIKED IT BEST WHEN _____
_____
_____

MY FAVORITE CHARACTER WAS _____
_____

I LIKED THIS CHARACTER BECAUSE _____
_____
_____

A DIFFERENT TITLE COULD BE _____
_____
_____

IF I COULD CHANGE THE ENDING, I WOULD _____
_____
_____

134

THE BOY BATHING
Give Help When It's Needed and Advice When It's Asked

THE BOY BATHING

CAST OF CHARACTERS:

Boy
Mother
Old man
Children

A mother stood outside the house waving good-bye to her son, "Enjoy your friends on this balmy spring afternoon, but take care not to do anything foolish. We will look for your return at suppertime."

The boy turned around, calling back, "You have my promise, Mother." He reassured her, "My friends and I will fish, chase rabbits in the clearing beyond the forest, or look for turtles...I will do nothing to cause you concern."

He walked for quite awhile in search of his friends, since there was a great distance between neighbors in the countryside. "What a marvelous day to be outside," he thought. As he walked, the noon sun began to beat steadily upon his head. It warmed his face and neck and arms until finally he felt rivulets of sweat plastering his shirt to his back. It was indeed a most surprisingly hot day for spring.

"If I were to go to the lake nearby, perhaps I would find my friends there. It would be ever so nice just to dip my toes in the cooling water."

THE BOY BATHING

The boy knew very well that the heat and the lure of the water would make him do much more than just dip his toes. As if his feet knew the way, with no help from his brain, he found himself, at last, looking over the blue lake that matched the color of the sky. His friends were not there but he paused, sat on the shore and surveyed the water with its small tumbling rapids--so inviting. The air shimmered in the heat and the water beckoned to him.

Presently he sprang up. "I cannot resist," he said aloud. "My mother would understand--even though no one is around, even though it is too early to swim--my mother would understand that the heat forced me to cool myself."

Settling that matter to his satisfaction, he removed his outer clothing and plunged into the blue ripples and the bubbling white foam. He was quickly awash in the shocking cold of the spring water. A summer swim did not take one's breath away like this. He persisted with his paddling. He made believe he was a boat, a fish, a snake in the water, and he sang happily to himself:

"To swim like a fish
Is my fondest wish."

THE BOY BATHING

All at once he was aware that he was not having such a free and spirited swim. "This is no longer a pleasure. I feel myself drawn into a place which is far too swift and deep." One could easily see that something was terribly wrong. Just then a man who was walking on the shore came into view. With a great effort the boy raised his soaking head out of the water to shout, "Help, help! Please look this way!"

The man turned and was shocked at what he saw. "What business do you have swimming at this time of year? It is too early to swim! Are you dimwitted, you young fool?" The man shook his cane at the swimmer.

The boy seemed to descend deeper. "Save me, save me. Reason this out with me after you have rescued me!" But his cries seemed to be of no use, for the man, full of wrath, persisted.

THE BOY BATHING

"Do you know that swimming is not allowed here? I should report you to the authorities. You need to get a good whack with a stick!"

"I am satisfied that you are right in all you say," the boy gasped, "But how can I redeem myself if you let me drown?" His head disappeared under the water again.

The man hollered back righteously, "What kind of rascality is this? Keep your head above the water when I speak to you!"

Just then, and none too soon, a group of boys and girls overheard the commotion. They came running to the bank of the river. They reproached the man, "This is not the time for the boy to be scolded for his foolish act."

"He is drowning, don't you see?"

"He is nearly out of his senses."

In a giant outburst of splashing energy, the children all rushed into the water still wearing their shoes and stockings and trousers and skirts. They formed a human chain of helping hands to drag the boy out. He clung to them and they pulled him to the bank. He emerged onto the safety of the shore looking like a drenched rat.

When the boy caught his breath he thanked the children and wept for joy. For the man, however, he reserved his special rancor. To him he said, "I would gladly repent and change my bad ways, sir,--but could you not have saved my life first and given me advice later?"

The Point of the Story: Give help when it's needed and advice when it's asked.

Ideas to Dramatize and Discuss

1. To represent the act of moving in the water or swimming, have the main character and the children lie on the floor and move their arms and legs in slow motion. One can reach the surface, gasp for air or shout for help and then go under again in this posture.

2. Have the mother called to the riverbank. As mothers do, she cries loudly for the safety of her child. When he is rescued, she first embraces him and is thankful, but then harangues him, grabs him by the ear, and threatens him with punishment for misbehaving.

3. Try the entire skit in pantomime, in slow and bold movements, from beginning to end. The action is so real to life that it can be dramatized without a word and be completely understood.

4. The old man, instead of shaking his finger at the boy and giving him a lecture, takes off his shoes, hat and watch and jumps into the lake to rescue him. He realizes, when he is sinking, that he cannot swim. What happens?

5. As in so many folk tales, a large fish rescues the boy from the water but then demands strange payment. What will it be?

6. A constable of the law appears on the scene and wants to arrest the boy. She explains that it is against the law to place oneself in a dangerous situation. What does their conversation sound like?

7. Has there been a time you can remember when someone got you out of trouble and did not say "I told you so"?

Props to Use

Have actors wear signs identifying their characters. Post signs for any other information when needed to help the play.

= A vest and a large hat for the older man on the shore
= Water toys held by the children on the shore
= A long dress for Mother
= A rope on shore for rescuing people
= A rubber raft near the water
= An umbrella carried by a passerby in the park
= A big sign that says, "Danger! No Swimming!"

My Name _____

SHOWTIME SKILLS

THE NAME OF THE PLAY WAS _____
_____

CHARACTERS IN THE PLAY: ACTED BY:

_____   _____

_____   _____

_____   _____

_____   _____

• •

THE PLAY MADE ME FEEL _____
_____
_____

I LIKED IT BEST WHEN _____
_____
_____

MY FAVORITE CHARACTER WAS _____
_____
_____

I LIKED THIS CHARACTER BECAUSE _____
_____
_____

A DIFFERENT TITLE COULD BE _____
_____

IF I COULD CHANGE THE ENDING, I WOULD _____
_____
_____

THE RICH WOMAN AND HER RAGS
It Is Foolish to Get Attention for the Wrong Reasons

THE RICH WOMAN AND HER RAGS

CAST OF CHARACTERS:

Rich woman
Husband
Servants
Dressmaker and helpers
Market vendors

A rich woman, in these parts, was so vain that she needed constant attention to keep her happy. She would forever badger her servants into telling her about the especial charms of her person.

"How do I appear to you when I walk down the staircase?"

"Regal, dear madam, simply regal!"

"When I hold my face so--do my eyes engage your interest?"

"Fascinating I assure you, lovely mistress. Not another pair of eyes like those have I ever beheld!"

"When I alight from my carriage, do you see my elegant slippers just so?" she asked, looking down at a trim and slender ankle.

"Hands of gold must have fashioned such slippers. That is clear for all to see."

"Does my voice ring a bell in your heart when you hear me speak?"

"Quite so. Sweeter than the bells that chime in the church steeple, gracious lady."

THE RICH WOMAN AND HER RAGS

Hers was, you see, a most tiresome need! This lady had to be tended like a garden. Her husband assured her of her loveliness. Her servants were constant in their praise of her. Her friends, who cultivated her for her lavish entertainments, also flattered her unwaveringly. The lady's inordinate preoccupation with herself made her a most demanding person.

Her servants grumbled to one another. "The lady is so taken with herself. Will she never leave off with her need for puffery? She leaves us no time for our work!"

"Nor us to ours," lamented the downstairs servants. "She is like a young child who needs to be noticed and petted."

Now one day this vain, rich woman decided to indulge her wish for the most beautiful dress in the world so that she could garner even more attention. She took herself promptly to her dressmaker.

I want you to make a dress for me that will capture everyone's admiration, no matter where I may be."

THE RICH WOMAN AND HER RAGS

The dressmaker listened attentively and responded, "Since you are prepared to pay a handsome price for such a dress, I promise it shall be yours."

In due time the magnificient dress was made. The lady was fitted with care by the seamstress and her fluttering helpers. "Now I will test your work," the vain woman said. To everyone's great shock and amazement, she went directly to the open marketplace in the middle of town.

The booths and stalls were crowded with busy vendors and customers going about their daily concerns.

"Fresh fish, fresh fish here! See my carp and mullet."

"Rutabaga, leeks, tubers. Get your vegetables here."

The rich lady picked up her skirts as she minced about in the filth of the marketplace. She walked between, around and over the bushels and baskets of wares. Her head was held regally, as befitted her station. She maintained her dignity, but alas--no one noticed her!

THE RICH WOMAN AND HER RAGS

"There is not one eye upon me. Not a soul has looked at me or my dress! I shall go back to the seamstress and complain."

As the vain woman turned, the business of the market continued, uninterrupted. "Yeast breads, scones, muffins. Get your baked goods here."

The lady made her appearance at the dressmaker's once again. Her eyes smoldered with anger. She complained in a huff that the dress was a dismal failure.

"Not a soul, not a person, not a dog turned to notice me."

The dressmaker and her helpers tried again. This time they hung another elegant and fashionable gown upon the lady. Once again, she sallied forth to the marketplace. But the dismal scene was reenacted and once more she was denied the attention she yearned for.

"I have come back," she stormed at the poor seamstress," and I warn you that you shall pay dearly for another failure."

The rich woman fussed and fumed while the desperate dressmaker set about her strange task. "If it is attention at any cost that she wants in the marketplace, then she shall have as much as she wants."

THE RICH WOMAN AND HER RAGS

Everyone in the little shop scurried about collecting pieces of cloth of every hue and color, of every shape and shade, of every warp and woof. Finally, the dressmaker and her helpers did the unexpected! They pulled out the contents of a huge bag of rags and from this jumble and hodgepodge they fashioned the impossible woman a dress. It was--unlike--any other!

The conceited woman ventured out again to the marketplace. But this time every eye was upon her. Every face turned her way. Even the dogs and the children stopped and stared. For the grand dame was attired in the wildest, most outlandish and bizarre dress that even the poorest of the street people had ever seen. The skirt, the peplum, the sleeves, the bodice, the flounce were made entirely of rags. Rags--all rags. Imagine a garment made of rags. Onlookers snickered, they pointed, they laughed out loud! It was the very best of entertainment.

But, oh, how she strutted and warmed to their attention, because in her foolish vanity she was content. Now, at last, the rich woman had been truly noticed by everyone.

The Point of the Story: It is foolish to get attention for the wrong reasons.

Ideas to Dramatize or Discuss

1. As she stands silently, a farmer comes along and mistakes the rich woman for a scarecrow and tries to take her home. When she speaks, he believes she is a scarecrow that has come to life.
2. The woman's husband sees her in rags and is so angry with her nonsense that he tells her she is just a comic figure who makes people feel sorry for her. How does she defend herself? What does the argument sound like?
3. An orphan who is dressed in rags, because he is destitute, believes the woman must be his poor, lost mother. He rushes up to her joyously shouting, "Mother, Mother!" What is the conversation between them?
4. The rich lady is so humiliated by her experience that she learns an important lesson and changes her ways. Dramatize her change of attitude and personality.
5. Make a rag dress or a rag suit. Have a real live fashion show in the marketplace with an announcer to explain about the garments and the designers.
6. Have a news report of this fashion show in a society column. Have every student contribute one line to the story which will be read aloud on the evening news.
7. A storyteller comes along and reads or tells the story of "The Emperor's New Clothes," by Hans Christian Andersen. What are the similarities between the Aesop and Andersen stories?
8. What have you seen or heard that attracted attention, which you thought was really foolish?

THE RICH WOMAN AND HER RAGS

Props to Use

Have actors wear signs identifying their characters. Post signs for any other information when needed to help the play.

= A hand mirror for the lady to be looking into wherever she goes
= A stool for the woman to stand on in the dressmaker's shop
= A grownup's dress with patches sewn all over it
= Baskets, boxes, and filled plastic bags for the market scene
= Straw hats, kerchiefs, ties and long skirts for the market vendors
= A large backdrop of a person dressed in a ridiculous outfit, with polka dots, stripes and plaids

My Name _____

SHOWTIME SKILLS

THE NAME OF THE PLAY WAS _____
_____

CHARACTERS IN THE PLAY: ACTED BY:

_____   _____
_____   _____
_____   _____
_____   _____
_____   _____

* *

THE PLAY MADE ME FEEL _____
_____
_____

I LIKED IT BEST WHEN _____
_____
_____

MY FAVORITE CHARACTER WAS _____
_____

I LIKED THIS CHARACTER BECAUSE _____
_____

A DIFFERENT TITLE COULD BE _____
_____

IF I COULD CHANGE THE ENDING, I WOULD _____
_____
_____

PROP COLLECTION

This is a starter list of suggestions for props, some of which can be kept in the room as a steady source for playacting. The children can be marvelously ingenious in working out uses for all manner of odds and ends and old clothes.

coffee cup	broom	toy phone
bowl	eyeglasses	ladder
wig	binoculars (two o.j. cans)	boots
spoon, fork	sheet	shoes
stool	pillowcase	mustache
doll	tablecloth	beard
shawl	cane	packing materials
tools	umbrella	boxes

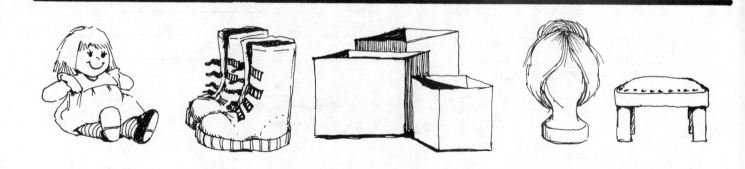

plastic bowl	small pillow	bucket
skillet	belts	fishing rod
teapot	curtains	stuffed toys
long socks	ties	crutches
earrings, other jewelry	ribbons	potholders
sweaters	gloves	bags (plastic and super-market)
coats	yarn	scarf
vase	fake flowers	towels
bottles	hats of all kinds (rain, baseball, sailor, cowboy, helmet)	suspenders
candlesticks		adult clothes (shirts, dresses, skirts)

JUNK PLAYS

With a prop box in the room, the teacher has a steady, rich source for seeding improvisational plays. Divide the children into groups. Give each group a choice of five randomly selected items from the box. Allow the children adequate conference time to create a play based upon the items they have chosen. The challenge to their creativity can be inspirational--the results amazing!

NOTES ON DRAMA AWARD

===

Dear Colleague:

With any award or acknowledgment of a child's effort, the teacher supports those qualities which are valued in that classroom and are worthy of praise. Among these achievements are not only all the language arts skills, but social skills that contribute to a good learning environment! In filling out the following award certificate, it is possible to include everyone!

The **CLASSROOM DRAMA AWARD** may be given to anyone in the class. It is a recognition of the following contributions to the creative drama enterprise. Here are just a few behaviors which merit reward:

Cooperation	Taking a Chance	A Great Laugh
Good Listening	Clever Props	Thoughtful Acts
Oral Expression	Artwork	Appreciation of Others
Creativity	Fun Ideas	Heartfelt Applause
Kind Criticism	Patience	Storytelling Ability
Acting	Helpfulness	Good Reading
Writing	Courtesy	Excellent Suggestions
Narrating	Imaginative Makeup	Attentiveness

===

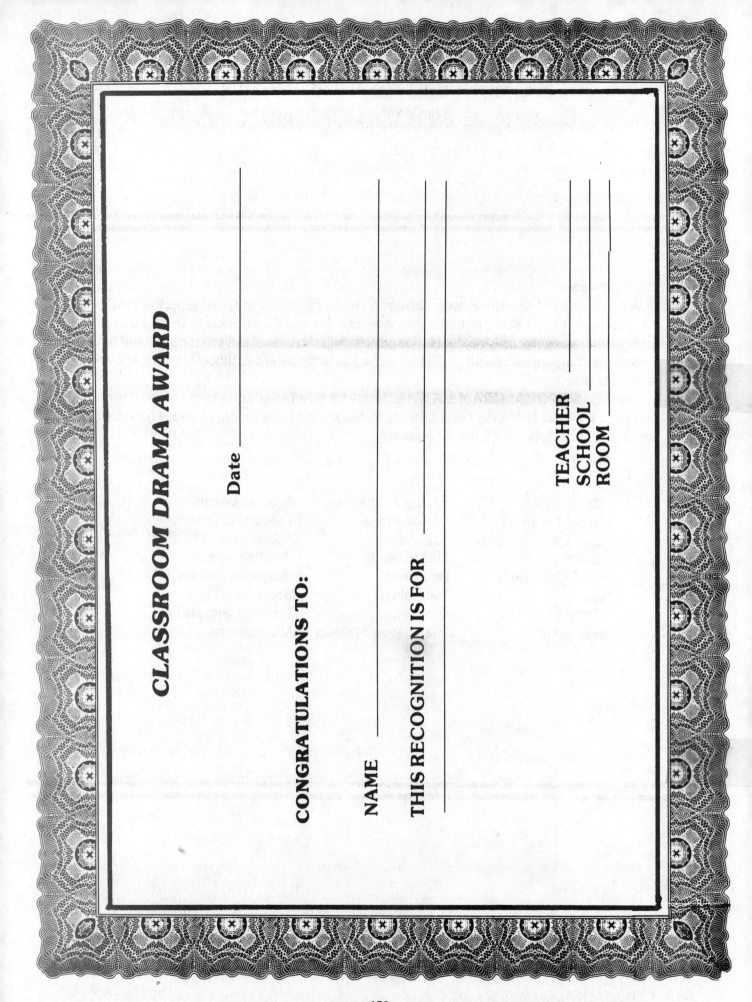

CLASSROOM DRAMA AWARD

Date _____

CONGRATULATIONS TO:

NAME _____

THIS RECOGNITION IS FOR _____

TEACHER _____
SCHOOL _____
ROOM _____